Fated Mates

OF THE

DRAKOAN

SEASON 1: JESS & DAVIN

DANIELLE FORREST

The Eternal Scribe Publishing
Indianapolis, IN

FATED MATES OF THE DRAKOAN: SEASON 1

Jess and Davin

DANIELLE FORREST

PRONUNCIATIONS & DEFINITIONS

PRONUNCIATIONS

- Drakoan - Drah-coh-in
- Drakonian - Drah-coh-nee-in
- Drakon - Drah-gun
- Koa - Goh-ah

DEFINITIONS

- Drakoan (n.) - species of red, scaled alien that are currently allied with humans
- Drakonian (adj.) - being the possession of or containing characteristics of Drakoans.
- Drakon (n.) - a shifted form of Drakoans which is a direct consequence of biological mating.
- Koa (n.) - the Drakonian homeworld.

EPISODE ONE

The Problem with Earth

---

*H*e stared down at a list of names, the information in front of him overwhelming. Name after name stared back at him, along with country of origin, popularity, pronunciation, spelling variants, and so much more. He nearly growled with frustration.

You just need to pick one.

It felt weird, just picking a name like this. He'd been putting this off, just going by "commander" when talking with the human ships, but that wasn't exactly a long-term solution. He *had* to pick a name if he wanted to interact with humans with any regularity. They didn't have the oral capacity to pronounce many Drakonian names, and from what he could tell, it was a time-honored tradition for foreigners on Earth to pick local names. And he supposed it *was* easier to learn to identify with a name people could pronounce than to wince every time people butchered your birth name.

With resignation, he scrolled down with his eyes closed and tapped his finger on the screen, then peeked one eye open.

Davin.

"I guess I'm Davin now." He sighed and switched screens on his monitor, returning to the impetus that had finally forced him to pick a name—the situation with Earth. His fleet and the remainder of the human military ships surrounding the planet had been trying to contact Earth command for days now, too many days, and they were growing concerned.

No, that wasn't true. They had long passed the point of "concerned." No one said it, but he could see the panic rising in the eyes of the captains of the other ships when they had their conference calls. *Everyone* was worried. *No one* knew what was going on down there.

As he continued reviewing what little information they had, he tried to reassure himself that everything was probably fine. From what he could tell, those last bombs, the ones that had turned the tides of the conflict, had also deactivated or destroyed every satellite in orbit. He could communicate with the other ships, but his files indicated that a massive amount of the Earth's communication systems relied on that satellite network which was now defunct.

His comm buzzed, startling him and jerked his mind away from his concerns for the people of Earth. "Damn it," he said, copying a common Earth phrase he'd learned while watching their media back home. He'd grown up with it, after all. While the streaming services had set up shop on Koa for the human colony there, they'd quickly become quite popular among the Drakoans as well.

Davin looked down at his bracer, internally groaning when his sister's name scrolled across the screen. He tapped answer, and the bracer interfaced with his desk, putting the video up on the monitor. She smiled at him in that enigmatic way she had, and he knew something was up.

He sighed. "What did you do?"

She clutched her chest, pretending to be offended. Light glinted off pale red scales she'd clearly spent a sizable portion of the day polishing and primping to perfection. "Me? I can't believe you'd say such a thing."

Davin didn't speak, instead crossing his arms and waiting for the inevitable confession. He was reminded of why he spent so much time away from home. His family was chaos incarnate and joining the *military* had been the only way to get a little peace in his life.

Of course, chaos could never let peace reign for long, and today was no different.

Eventually, she gave up the pretense. "It wasn't me." She looked away from the camera, her gaze roving around the room, and he just *knew* she was trying to come up with some excuse that would shift the blame away from one of her nightmarish kids. Because why else would she be calling? It certainly wasn't to talk to *him*. "My son was playing in your room earlier today."

Davin's entire body went tense, and he saw red. "My room is off limits. You know that." It took everything in him to keep still. He wanted to yell, to pace, but a fit of anger wouldn't solve anything, especially not with *his* family.

"Oh, you know kids. Can't keep them out of anything," she said, waving her hand in dismissal.

Yeah, especially when you unlock the door for the little monsters.

He could just see it now. His nephew had probably been whining and generally being a pain, and instead of actually parenting him, she'd bribed him with exploring the forbidden, aka his uncle's locked room. "What happened?"

She held up an action figure that was currently missing an arm. "It was an accident."

Davin ground his teeth and closed his eyes, trying to regain control.

Anger doesn't solve anything. Besides, you can't strangle her over a comm.

He opened them again and forced words out through gritted teeth. "That… was a Star Wars Limited Edition. I bought it when I was ten." It was one of his most prized possessions. Growing up, he'd been obsessed with Star Wars. There had been other "Science Fiction" shows and movies to watch, but many had steered a little too close to the familiar, a little too close to home. But Star Wars? Star Wars was different. It involved special powers and the ultimate fight of good vs. evil. For a little boy, the idea of playing around with a light sword and moving things with your mind? Pure magic.

As he'd grown older, he'd started collecting. It was hard coming by these things, partially because he lived on another planet and partially because Star Wars was a very old franchise and thus a fairly niche one. Not everyone had even heard of it, and that made wanting to collect all things Star Wars even more important to him. He couldn't enthuse about it with his friends, and so he'd thrust those impulses into his treasures.

As he'd grown up, those impulses had matured, and eventually, they'd even been part of the reason he'd decided to join the military. The idea of being like the Jedis was appealing to him. He liked the idea of being a hero, of being on the front lines, of maybe even being the only thing between peace and war.

She waved her hand again. "I know how much you like your silly Star something or 'nother, but it was just an accident. You know he didn't mean anything by it."

He looked away.

There she goes again. Opens her mouth and suddenly I'm pissed.

"It wasn't an accident," he ground out. "It shouldn't have been within his reach. The door was locked for good reason. I don't want anyone touching my things. You know this."

"Oh, it's not that big a deal."

"Isn't it? You encourage him to violate someone's privacy, their personal space, then you try to prevent him from having consequences when he damages another person's property, which is a crime, by the way."

She glared at him, her expression growing calculating. "Do I have to get mom on the line?"

For a split second, his heart lurched in his chest, his immediate reaction of panic setting in before he could control it. "Mom" was the ultimate authority, and each of his generation wielded it like a finely hewn weapon to be unleashed with ruthlessness. "You're lucky I don't have the time for this. Lives are on the line, and I need to go," he said, changing the subject.

"Aren't they always?" A slight smirk tipped her lips. "Well, I said what I intended to say. I'll catch you later."

She ended the call, and he fell back in his seat with a groan, palm covering his eyes. "Family sucks." A part of him wished he could go home and inspect his room. What else had the little monster got into while he was breaking things? Just thinking about the possibilities sent anxiety spiking through him.

I need to upgrade my locks.

He took several deep breaths, then pulled up the messenger app on his desk.

Hello, Mom. Can you upgrade the locks on my room?
And this time, don't give my sister a key. My nephew
got in there again.

He hit send and let out a deep breath. "It's so much easier to talk to her over text," he said, shaking his head and chuckling at the contradictions. He loved his mom, loved his family, but most of the time, he needed at least a few hundred thousand miles between them just to stay sane.

"Now, where was I?" He checked the open screens on his computer. "Right." He returned to staring at information that had started to blur together and almost made *less* sense the more he reviewed it. And the longer the situation persisted, the tighter the knots in his stomach grew. The unknown was a terrible thing, and knowing that the fate of an entire planet, an entire species, was unknown? He didn't even want to *think* about what all could be going on down there. It was too much to contemplate.

Knock, knock, knock.

He looked up at his office door. "Enter."

His second in command stepped in, shoulders pulled back and chin high. Behind him, his tail was perfectly still, speaking to the reserved presence he was known for.

"Have you picked a human name yet?"

"Van," he said with a nod, his line of a mouth growing even thinner. It was the closest thing to a frown he'd ever seen on the man.

"Good. Have we heard from the humans again?"

"I talked with the Captain of the USS Venture."

"And?" Davin leaned forward, eager for news. They'd come to back up Earth's defenses against an alien invasion days ago, only to find destruction. A shiver ran up his spine as he remembered the devastation. A massive debris field had cluttered the space around the planet, with only a handful of human ships still registering on the bridge's display. Around those ships, countless unidentified orange dots had surrounded them, and for a heart-stopping moment, he'd wondered if his fleet had arrived too late.

But moments later, an explosion had detonated unlike anything he'd ever seen. His people were mostly peaceful, keeping to themselves, keeping a standing military exclusively for defensive purposes. He'd never seen anything like it. He'd believed it impossible. That is, until that blindingly-white light blotted out their cameras and shorted their displays, throwing the room into perfect darkness.

They'd scrambled to get their systems back online while fearing for their allies. With no working cameras, sensors, or comms, all they'd had was their imaginations to fill in the blanks. It wasn't until later, when they'd reestablished contact with the other ships, that they'd learned that Earth Command had detonated a nuclear bomb.

Many nuclear bombs.

"The satellites are a lost cause," Van said, interrupting Davin's thoughts.

"Oh?" he said, tuning back into the conversation. It had been easy of late to let his mind wander. There were just too many unknowns in this situation, and he didn't like it. His mind wanted to run through tactics and scenarios, plan out strategies for each potential eventuality, but the possibilities were limitless and there was only so much time.

"The Venture's Captain sent shuttles to investigate if they could salvage any of the satellites, but a significant percentage of them have already lost geostationary orbit. Many more will require extensive repair and some, they haven't been able to find. He thinks they were destroyed in the blasts."

Davin nodded. "And that means there's no hope of communicating with Earth?"

In an uncharacteristic expression of emotion, Van sighed. "It means communication is more… difficult. As we've been able to confirm, their communications systems *are* designed around those satellites. But the captain's also concerned that there could be broader issues at play."

"Like?"

"The planet's gone dark."

Davin tensed. "Gone dark?"

"Yes. During their investigations, shuttles that traveled to the night side of the planet reported no electrical lighting visible from space."

Meaning they've lost power.

"So," Davin said, "even if we had the satellites up and running, there's no guarantee anyone could respond."

"That was my conclusion as well," Van said with a nod of respect.

"Contact the human captains again. I want a conference call."

"You have a plan?" Van asked.

"When do I not?"

Van paused, waiting for the explanation he knew was coming.

"Someone has to go down to Earth, reestablish contact. Without the satellites or power, there's no way to even *try* to do it from here." He shook his head, worry for the humans intensifying. What was happening down there? Were they okay? And had any of the enemy managed to slip past them before the blasts? He hadn't really thought of that yet, but it was possible, right? There was no guarantee *all* the enemy had been destroyed. *Anything* could be going on down there. *Nothing* was outside the realm of possibility at this point.

"And you intend it to be us."

Davin nodded. "I do." He couldn't imagine doing it any other way. Maybe it was a failing of his, but he'd always believed if you wanted something done right, you didn't ask someone else to do it.

Van stiffened. "They could shoot at us. They just fought off an alien invasion. You know how humans can be."

He did. He'd seen enough human movies and shows to know sometimes their modus operandi was "shoot first, ask questions later," but he didn't care. The humans needed help, and he wanted to help them.

And there was no one he trusted to do that more than his own people.

avin tried to keep a neutral expression as he entered the shuttle bay.

Head tall.

Shoulders back.

Exude confidence.

He was a leader, a commander. The team he'd chosen might have been his closest friends, but they were also his subordinates. He could never forget that, and it meant constantly balancing how he felt personally against the needs of his position.

Sometimes, he wondered if it was worth it.

Van stood by the shuttle, a small smile on his face as he oversaw the team. Other teams were also rushing around the shuttle bay, preparing for their own missions. Each of the ships in the fleet would have a similar scene playing out in their own shuttle bays.

Coordinating with the human captains, they'd settled on a plan. His teams would send down shuttles to the planet's surface, to each of the most influential governing centers, and reestablish communication while the human crews would work up here in space to repair and replace the technology that had been damaged or destroyed. Hopefully, between their combined efforts, they would find some semblance of normalcy again.

At least they probably didn't have to worry about the enemy. He still wasn't entirely sure what species had attacked Earth's forces in the first place, but when their systems had come back online, there had been nothing left of them. The bombs had done their jobs thoroughly. The Earth's last ditch effort to save itself had worked, but had come at a great cost. As yet, they didn't know *how* great.

His team continued flitting in and out of the shuttle, prepping it for their mission.

"Status," he said as he came up beside Van.

"Almost ready, Commander."

He nodded. "Anything else from the Venture?"

"No, Commander, but any future calls will be relayed through the shuttle to our comms." He tapped his bracer as he spoke. The bracer was the most high-tech gadget any of them generally kept on their persons. Civilian versions were smaller, less than half as wide, but for the military, it covered most of the forearm. It was their comms, their mission computer, their everything.

"All set, Commander," a deep feminine voice barked from the back of the shuttle. Her deep red scales shimmered in the overhead lighting.

"Excellent. Let's get started."

The team quickly stomped up the ramp, which started closing behind them. Davin continued forward, slipping quickly through the gear room at the back of the shuttle and into the main hallway. He passed by bunkrooms on either side and a tiny med bay on the right before entering the bridge. It was much smaller than the ship's bridge, with only enough seats for the six of them. Their pilot was already in his seat, his hands touching screens, buttons, and switches as he prepared for launch. The only woman on the team plopped down beside him, opening up the communications display. The rest of them settled into the four remaining seats, securing themselves in their harnesses with practiced ease.

Unsurprisingly, their chatty, if blunt, CO immediately turned around in her seat and started talking, "So, what names did everyone pick? I picked Grace."

Someone in the room snorted.

Grace turned, glaring at their Tech Officer.

"I picked Heath," his pilot said, ever the peacekeeper, trying, as always, to distract Grace before all hell broke loose.

"Lane," their quiet Weapons Officer said.

"Van."

Their TO snorted again, shaking his head.

"What's so funny?" Grace snapped, losing her cool as the engines roared to life.

Davin frowned. Grace *should* have been communicating with the shuttle bay crew, informing them they were ready for launch. Instead, she was shooting daggers at their TO with her eyes.

"You all picked like objects and shit," he said, snorting again.

She renewed her glare, looking like she was about to release her harness and tackle him, which wouldn't end well. While their TO was much larger than her, she had a tendency to fight dirty and wasn't averse to using her claws when she felt like it. "And what did *you* pick?"

Their TO puffed up a little before speaking. "Erik. A nice, normal, human name."

Grace rolled her eyes, but finally turned back around and opened a comm line.

Sitting next to him, Van looked over at Davin, shaking his head like a long suffering parent dealing with a recalcitrant child. Conversely, Davin smiled, struggling with the urge to laugh. As a commander, he had to maintain a certain amount of distance, but he savored moments like this, even when he couldn't participate himself. He remembered how he used to joke around with his cohorts. There was something special about relationships in the military, a closeness and bond you couldn't experience anywhere else. He kind of missed it. These people were his closest friends, but other than Van, he couldn't really express himself the way he wished. He would love to join in on their banter, but it wouldn't be professional.

He let out a quiet sigh as the bay doors began opening before them. The shuttle lifted off, and they blasted forward, the inertia pushing Davin into his seat. In mere moments, the front shield grew red with the heat of entry, and he gripped his seat as a part of him thrilled at the ride.

Her job done, Grace tilted her head back and said, "So, what did you choose, Commander?"

"Davin."

The red began to fade and the details of the planet's surface came into view. From here, everything looked oddly flat. He could just barely make out landmasses and bodies of water with clouds still marring the view, but little else.

She nodded, pausing only briefly before opening her mouth again. "So, what do you guys know about humans?"

There was a moment of silence before anyone said anything, the topic change both jarring and wholly expected from Grace at this point.

"Probably as much as you," Heath said, elbowing her from the pilot's seat with an irreverent grin plastered on his face. "I bet as soon as you found out about this mission to Earth, you started researching their mating practices."

"Shut up, you tail licker," she said with a frown as she punched him in the arm.

He only laughed, ignoring her punch as he continued piloting the shuttle.

After mumbling something under her breath, she slouched in her seat and crossed her arms. "So what if I want to get mated someday? Is that so wrong? At least I'm not a hypocrite about it," she said, turning around to glare at the rest of the team accusingly. "You all are just too cowardly to admit it."

The fact that no one balked at being called a coward was answer enough. Mating was a quirk of their biology, an urge that, before modern medicine, was uncontrollable, stealing a Drakoan's sanity, practically devolving them into animals. It was archaic, and most of their society frowned on it, even though it was rare in the first place. And yet still, some like Grace yearned for it. Many called it just biology, but for some it was romantic, like fate touching two people and nudging them together.

Davin, personally, had never really thought about it. Between his family and his career, he had little time to find a partner, let alone long for a mate. Not that he needed one. Who had time for that when you had parents, grandparents, siblings, cousins, nieces, and nephews all living under the same roof? Sometimes it felt like he'd joined the military just to get some much needed peace and quiet.

"Approaching our landing vector," Heath said, jarring Davin out of his thoughts.

He looked up, a little alarmed to realize they were almost there, to realize he'd lost track of time.

But that wasn't the only thing that alarmed him. The plan had been to initially touch down just outside of Washington, D.C., then travel to New York City when they were done. The two cities were relatively close together, and both were significant on the global scale, one being the seat of the government of the United States of America and the other being the location of the United Nations Headquarters. Both were important targets for reestablishing contact.

And yet, as he looked out the front shield, he was shocked by what he saw. They were flying over a city of some sort, but it didn't look like the pictures he'd seen of Earth. There was smoke billowing into the air in places and instead of the clean streets he expected, filled with cars and people going about their lives, everything was quiet. No people. No moving cars. Where he could see details, he noticed signs of damage. Broken glass. Crumpled metal. Burn marks.

I thought the invasion didn't reach Earth.

And yet as he continued to stare down at the scene unveiling around him, a sick, twisting feeling in his gut told him they'd missed something. Something important. Something vital.

What the hell happened here?

EPISODE THREE

Smelling His Mate

"**S**tatus," Davin barked.

They had touched down in a clearing just outside of Washington, D.C. It was quiet, too quiet, and that left him on edge. They'd landed in the middle of a metropolitan area. It shouldn't be this quiet.

"Shuttle's locked down," Heath said as he stepped up to the group.

Grace looked down at her bracer. "Comms are good. Got a signal from the ship."

"Scans confirming distance and route to the US Capitol. Should take approximately one Earth hour," Erik said, looking down at his own bracer.

Davin nodded. He would have preferred parking closer. There was even a large lawn appropriate for landing in front of the White House. Unfortunately, the captain of the Venture had assured them that no unauthorized flights were allowed over Washington, D.C. airspace. If any of the normal systems were still in place, it could have caused an interplanetary incident and jeopardized their alliance, which was something he wasn't willing to risk.

Davin turned to Erik. "Good. Let's head out."

They quickly left the small park where they'd landed the shuttle, stepping into a residential area as they followed the route Erik had planned to their destination. At first, he almost forgot how things had appeared from the air. The buildings looked similar to the database photos he'd seen, with clean facades, intact windows and entries, and roofs constructed in a way that reminded him of his own scales. Beyond that, each home seemed to have trees, small green spaces, and often a vehicle called a "car." Some homes were large, consistent with the size of homes back on Koa, though humans didn't use them in the same ways. They called them "apartments," and loaded them up with *many* families instead of just one. Humans *did* have buildings intended for single families, but they were bafflingly small. He couldn't imagine any family living in a place so tiny, but that was apparently normal here on Earth.

As they continued toward the capitol, he kept a keen eye on their surroundings, idly scanning for threats as well as answers. Initially, the only sign of something darker was the occasional vehicle sitting idle in the road. Sometimes, it would just be stopped and abandoned, while other times, it had hit something. Another car. A small box propped up on a post. A sign. It wasn't until they left this residential area and entered a business sector that the true depth of what had happened here made itself known.

"What the...," Grace said under her breath. She stepped up to a storefront, her fingers dancing over the broken glass in the window frame before turning around. "What happened here?"

Van stepped up next to her, his head pivoting on his neck as he looked inside. "It's been ransacked." He turned, his steady gaze taking in the area around them.

They stood in a parking lot overlooking a major road, with businesses lining either side and abandoned cars clogging up its five lanes.

"They've all been ransacked," Van said, pulling back from the window.

Davin stepped up to his second in command. "What are you thinking?"

"I'm thinking we need to pick up our pace."

Davin frowned. "You think there are threats."

Van gave him his most penetrating stare. "I think we should be on our guard and expect the unexpected. At some point in the last few days, anarchy clearly took over here." He looked up and around once again. "If that happens again, we'd be outnumbered and overwhelmed."

Davin nodded. Van wasn't wrong. While the street was quiet now, that didn't mean it would stay that way. Cities on Earth had far denser populations than on Koa. There were likely *millions* of people within even a reasonable walking distance from their current location. He looked around him, at his team, his friends, people he was responsible for and cared about. A chaotic mix of emotions rose up inside him and he ruthlessly pushed it down, deeming it a dangerous distraction. He needed to focus, to keep his wits about him. He needed to get the job done and get out of here.

"Move out, everyone," he said, relieved to hear that none of the emotion he was currently feeling had slipped into his voice.

"Yes, Commander," they all said.

After that, he pushed them forward at a ruthless pace, always jogging or running, never stopping. Davin wanted to focus on where they were going, on getting to their destination, but he couldn't help the small inkling of paranoia that had slipped in. He was compelled to scan constantly for threats as they crossed a bridge and then eventually spotted the U.S. Capitol Building in the distance.

Almost there.

Then a brief gust of wind hit him in the face, and suddenly, he couldn't move. His entire body *screamed* that something important had just happened, but his brain was too slow to tell him *what.* He looked around, trying to figure out what he'd picked up on, but there was nothing. Just abandoned cars, damaged storefronts, and an eerie stillness that set his nerves on edge.

"Commander?" Van asked. He'd stopped and turned around to face Davin, a confused expression on his face.

"I…" he started to say, but he quickly closed his mouth again when no words came to mind. What *could* he say? That some ephemeral sense was holding him frozen to the spot? That even though he hadn't the slightest clue what he'd picked up on, he knew it was *vitally* important that he chase it down, that he solve the riddle of its existence? It had been there and gone so quickly. The only thing his brain had registered was just how *significant* it was. It felt like the air he breathed, the very blood in his veins. It felt *that* important, and yet he couldn't have even told you a single thing to describe it.

He shook his head in frustration and tried to ignore that nagging sense of significance as he looked up at Van. "It's nothing," he said, even though he didn't actually believe *anything* he'd just said.

Van, never willing to let things go, just arched a single eyebrow at him, telling him without a sound how little he believed Davin's words.

"I…" he started again, trying to put into words the weird feeling he had. The rest of the team was still jogging to their destination, leaving enough distance between them now for a private conversation.

But then the wind picked up again, and this time it wasn't just a brief gust. It was sustained and that vague sense of importance suddenly had substance. He could *smell* it, and it smelled exactly as it had always been described in all the books. It was enticing, compelling, and sweet enough to make his mouth water. His jaw hung open, and he struggled to breathe. He needed to expel air to take in his next breath, but all his body wanted to do was breathe *in*, to absorb as much of this manna as physically possible.

The emotion was so strong he almost felt like crying. In fact, he could feel the tears welling up in his eyes. "I…" he said again, his voice cracking with everything he was feeling.

"Davin?" Van said, this time looking worried as he slowly approached. "Are you okay?"

You need to answer.

You need to tell him.

But his body and mind were struggling, caught between savoring this momentous event and performing the tiny acts necessary for survival. Then finally, something snapped and he let out a breath, gasping several times as his breathing returned to normal. He could still smell her, though, that sweet, addictive scent caressing his senses.

She's out there.

She's waiting.

He looked over at Van, now a profound sense of awe rushing through him. "Mate," he said under his breath, the very word feeling too divine for anything but a whisper.

"What?" Van said, walking closer, almost within reach now. "Davin, what is it?"

"She's here."

"Who, Davin? Who's here? You're not making any sense."

"My mate."

A FEW HOURS EARLIER…

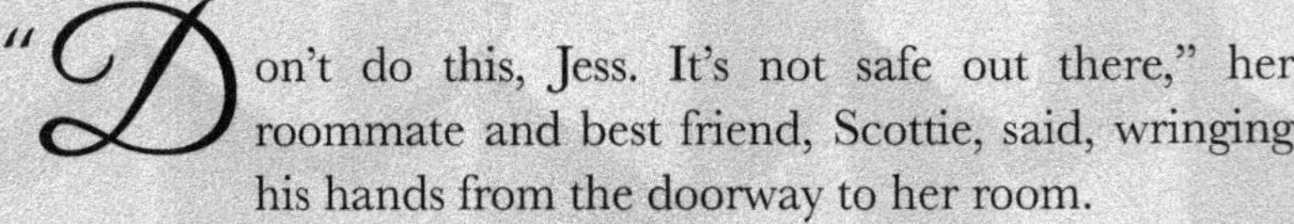

"*D*on't do this, Jess. It's not safe out there," her roommate and best friend, Scottie, said, wringing his hands from the doorway to her room.

She turned to him with a sigh. "Not now, Scottie." He was wearing one of his favorite Star Trek t-shirts and a pair of jeans that now had mud stains on the knees from working in Inez's garden.

Before everything had gone dark, not a single one of them would have even *dreamed* of invading her garden. That was *her* space, *her* sanctuary, and they'd all respected that. They all had their own passions and projects, their own interests, and that was what made their household, filled with six young adults, all starting out their respective careers, work.

But now? Worry left everyone feeling the need to *do* something. And with no power, no work, and a cloud of paranoia and fear hovering over them, they sometimes ended up invading each other's private spaces and boundaries. She

22

wished she could say she was the exception, but she'd also offered to help in the garden more than a couple times since everything went haywire.

Hell, just the fact that she was even *contemplating* this course of action probably said a lot about their situation. She didn't necessarily *want* to leave, but it was starting to become claustrophobic, and she was starting to worry about their supplies.

No, that was a lie. She'd been worrying about their supplies for a while now. Six adults could plow through some food pretty quickly, and the first thing to go in the stores had been the food. It had all started when the government had announced the alien siege. The government had told people not to panic, to stay in their homes as much as possible. A State of Emergency had been declared. People *should* have stayed home, chewing on their nails as they obsessively watched the broadcasts, waiting on the news of their own salvation or destruction.

Instead, Americans being Americans, they'd felt compelled to *do* something, even when there was nothing to do. The next thing you knew, the shelves were empty, and you saw people rolling shopping carts away from the grocery stores with more food than any one family could use in a lifetime. It was wasteful and left most people going without, but that didn't stop people from doing it anyway.

She and her roommates had spent that time inventorying their supplies, figuring out what would keep and what should be eaten first. Fortunately, they'd always kept a decent amount of canned goods on hand because, again, six young adults could wipe out a pantry at lightning speed. They'd figured they were good, that they could handle whatever came next so long as no one binged.

Then the power went out.

At first, they'd still thought everything would be fine. The recent communal panic had already put them in a good place for a power outage. Supplies were inventoried; flashlights, lighters, and candles were set out in each room; and the weather was temperate enough lately that they didn't have to worry about heat or cold.

Jess remembered calling out to each of her roommates, checking that everyone was okay. They'd all met in the living room. Scottie had complained about his game cutting out and losing his progress while Melissa had made a joke about having a slumber party.

Thom, ever thoughtful, slow to speak Thom, had cut the joke abruptly short when he'd said, "The phones don't work." He'd been holding his cell phone in his hand, looking down at it with a frown on his face.

"What do you mean?" Inez had said, reaching up to the little cross necklace she'd received at her Confirmation.

Thom had looked up and lifted his phone so all of them could see. The screen had been dark. "It won't power on."

And cell phones run on batteries.

Melissa had scoffed, flipping her hair off her shoulder as she spoke. "You probably just forgot to charge it."

"Then try yours," he'd said.

Jess and the other four roommates had then each pulled out their phones. Hers, Melissa's, and Scottie's had been in their pockets. Amanda's had been in the kitchen while Inez had left hers in her room. But within moments, they'd all been back, all staring down at their phones.

All the screens had been dark.

Jess remembered mashing the power button over and over

again. She remembered pushing the force-reset combination until her fingers hurt.

It didn't make a difference.

All the phones were dead.

"How is this possible? What does this mean?" Inez had asked, a slight quiver in her voice.

It was what they all had been thinking, what they all had been wondering, and no one truly had an answer.

"Surely, the government would say something," Melissa had said, her usual confidence and snark suddenly absent.

"What if they can't?" Thom had replied.

That was the thought that had been ringing through Jess's brain ever since that conversation.

What if they can't?

That thought had kept her from leaving the house. It was terrifying, paralyzing, and a part of her hadn't been ready to know yet. *Still* wasn't ready to know. She wanted to stay put, as the government had said, "stay in your homes." She wanted to pretend that this was all normal, that sometime soon they would get the power back up or that someone would start going through the neighborhoods with a bullhorn, telling them everything would be fine, giving them instructions on what to do next.

God, how she wished someone would tell her what to do.

And maybe that was part of the reason she was doing this, this thing that Scottie was begging her not to do. Maybe she just wanted someone to save her from the unknown. She looked over at Scottie, where he was still wringing his hands. His eyes beseeched her, begging her to stay.

"I have to do this."

"You don't. We'll be fine."

Jess gave him a dirty look. "We won't be fine. You know that as well as I do. We're burning through food fast, and if there's no power, I doubt we'll have clean running water for much longer. We need answers or we need supplies."

"We have supplies. Canned goods, the garden."

She paused, letting him absorb the seriousness of their situation. "We both know how long that's gonna last. The garden will only produce for so long, and the canned goods will be gone long before that. Inez's garden was never intended to feed us all, and it won't get us through the winter."

"We're nowhere near the winter. This will be solved before then."

"Will it? Seriously? Don't you know your history? Blackouts don't last this long! And they don't affect cell phones!" She flung her hands out to the sides. "We're already in uncharted territory here! We have no idea what's going to happen! We can't count on anything, not without information. And we have *no* information."

"You think you can learn something?"

Jess shook her head and shrugged. "I don't know. It's a long walk to the Capitol, but doable in a day. I've got my bow, a knife, and enough martial arts training that I can probably defend myself. I'll be fine. I'd rather try and fail than do nothing, though."

He fidgeted in place, thinking for several moments before finally giving in and saying, "Maybe you should bring some camping gear, just in case."

"No, if I have to be gone that long, I'll just stay awake. I don't know enough about what's going on to risk sleeping in the open."

Scottie's hand-wringing grew more agitated. "Maybe I should go with you."

Jess smiled, making an effort not to laugh. "No offense, Scottie, but you're probably the last person I'd want having my back in a fight."

He pouted, practically confirming her point. He wasn't a small man, necessarily, but he was more likely to exercise to look like a Klingon than to learn self defense.

"I'll be fine," she said, trying to reassure him.

"But you'll be leaving the neighborhood. There's no telling what it's like out there."

"I know. And I can always turn back. I'll be fine."

He looked down, then away, showing his defeat without words. Jess's chest tightened a little, compassion for her friend tying her in knots, but no matter how much she wanted to indulge him, they couldn't keep going like this. She turned her back, shifting her focus to the things she'd collected on her bed. Hydration backpack, plastic trash bags, a meal bar, a hunting knife, a quiver, her recurve bow, and a dozen arrows her father had bought her years ago. They were wicked sharp, and she shuddered even looking at them. He'd bought them hoping to take her hunting with him someday, but she'd always stalled him, saying she wasn't good enough yet. In reality, she'd been afraid, but also sympathetic. Most wild animals nowadays had to struggle to even find somewhere to live, let alone thrive. What right did she have to take that away from them when she could just buy food at the grocery store instead?

She quickly loaded her pack, slinging it on her back, then hesitated, her hands shaking a little when she reached for the arrows. She deviated, grabbing the knife instead, something she figured she probably wouldn't even have cause to use. It clipped securely at her waist, the sheathed blade pressing firmly against her outer thigh. Next was the quiver, the arrows, the moment of truth.

Why am I being so dramatic?

After all, what was the worst thing that could happen? She could chicken out. Or fail to find anything to hunt. She could miss.

I could actually kill something and just curl up into a ball, bawling all over its small, bloody corpse.

Yeah, that was probably likely. But hunting wasn't the only reason she was leaving the house. She couldn't forget that. They needed answers as much as they needed food right now. If they knew what was going on, how long they had to hold out, it would make a difference. They would know how to portion their meals. They would know if they needed to ration even further. No one had expected this to go on as long as it had already.

Her stomach churned with anxiety as she fisted the shafts of the arrows and slid them into her quiver. It was a cheap thing, something that was good enough for practicing in the backyard, but that wasn't really designed for travel. It clipped at her waist, dangling precariously. She shook her head at the terrible design. All the arrows would probably spill out onto the ground if she so much as leaned forward. In the past, it would have been fine. Today, she could feel its inadequacy.

Jess paused for a moment, staring at the last thing on the bed, her bow. There was something about it sitting there all alone, like it was an exclamation point on a sentence or maybe an accusation. It was stark against the plain blue comforter, its pale wood standing out in perfect contrast. She felt almost like the people in the movies in those scenes right before the action starts. She could practically hear the music egging her on.

She reached for the bow, a sick feeling twisting in her gut. Her hand pressed down on the riser, holding there for a moment. She closed her eyes, took a deep breath, then slowly curled her fingers around the smooth wood. Letting her anxiety settle, she slowly let out the breath, opened her eyes, and turned. Scottie was still there, now chewing his lip as well as wringing his hands.

Poor guy.

She took a deep breath and shook her head, then walked past him and out of her room, quickly jogging down the steps to the front door. No one else confronted her. She could just barely hear voices coming from the backyard, where they were likely "helping" Inez with her garden.

It was a comforting sound, something that almost made her forget that the world was ending. How could anything bad be happening when her friends were joking around out back?

But when she reached for the door handle, the cold bulb of metal pressing against her palm, one final moment of fear and doubt settled in.

What if it's dangerous out there?

She had no idea what had happened after everything died. They'd talked amongst themselves and later talked with their neighbors out front, but it was all speculation. Nobody had any news, not even Thom, and he worked for a congresswoman.

Not anymore.

The anxiety in her stomach amplified. None of them were working anymore.

And what if the government's gone?

What if there's anarchy out there?

She imagined a *Mad Max*-style post-apocalyptic landscape and shuddered.

"That's not what's happening here," she said, trying to reassure herself.

But what if the aliens have invaded?

That gave her pause. She hadn't heard *that* much about the aliens before the lights went out, only that a fleet of ships had amassed in Earth's orbit and that human forces were going to meet it and drive it back.

But what if they'd lost?

What if humans aren't in control anymore?

*J*ess pushed open the front door, and suddenly her feet froze in place, her entire body hesitant to take another step. The street was eerily quiet. There was no movement, and the only sound was the voices of her friends. In the garden out back, they were arguing about a lack of tools.

Maybe I'll check in with a hardware store on the way, she thought to herself. A hardware store might not be thoroughly picked over yet, and if they were lucky, maybe they'd have seeds, too.

Just in case.

Jess shifted her grip on her bow and grabbed a single arrow from the quiver on her hip. The flimsy container wobbled back and forth awkwardly, but she tried to ignore it, notching the arrow in case she saw something worth hunting. She'd never hunted before, but it couldn't be that hard. Just good aim and timing, right?

And she wasn't completely ignorant. She knew, for example, that when shooting a deer, you always went for the quick kill. Not only was it more merciful, but it also prevented the animal from running and dying miles away from you, unre-trievable.

As she started to wander the neighborhood, she became slightly disoriented and forced herself to focus, pushing back the many invasive thoughts that had consumed her since the power went out. Not having turn-by-turn directions for the first time in God only knew how long was a major contributing factor in her disorientation. And as she took in her surroundings, she realized even the experience of *walking* was messing with her, the sensory landscape so different from when she was driving. It meant familiar landmarks felt almost surreal.

A couple times on her walk, she saw squirrels or rabbits, but none of them stuck around long enough for her to raise her bow, let alone shoot it.

It's not much meat, anyway.

But that wasn't much of a consolation. A few animals that size would probably be enough meat for a day, and that was still better than using up their stores. *Anything* was better than nothing, especially when they didn't know when their situation would change.

She scoffed, shaking her head at her thoughts. She couldn't even say "go back to normal" in her own head. It felt like an idea so farfetched at this point, it wasn't even worth thinking about.

Time passed slowly as she navigated the Maryland suburbs and by the time she crossed the bridge over the Anacostia River, she'd been gone for several hours. Again, it was weird walking it. She'd always crossed the river by car or bus, never on foot. At one point, she looked over the side, staring down at the running water. It was surprisingly blue. She wasn't expecting it to be so blue. She remembered reading tons of articles about the pollution in the river, seen plenty of photos of it looking murky and brown.

Maybe it's having a good day.

She laughed. It was such a ridiculous thing to think, and as she continued crossing the bridge, a smile now stretched her face as she shook her head. She stopped when she reached the other side, staring off to her right at the small wooded area around the Anacostia Riverwalk Trail. It was the last bit of green she would likely see for a while, everything ahead of her being city streets and buildings until she reached the US Capitol. She squinted down at the trees, wondering if she would have a better chance at finding game there. But with the way the roads were designed, she might have an easier time getting to those woods on the way back.

Jess turned, looking out over the streets and buildings in the distance. She remembered seeing images in college, even those taken only a few decades ago, that had shown vivid green spaces and trees in the distance. No more. Once she focused on the city proper, it was all pavement and tall buildings. Standing there on the ground, rather than driving by in a car, the difference was even more staggering. There *used* to be historical buildings with quaint architecture, but now the skyline was filled with skyscrapers meant to overcome the multiple housing crises the area had experienced over the years.

She started walking down the street again, giving up on her quest for supplies for the moment in favor of answers. Right now, she suspected answers would serve them better, anyway. They still had food, after all. They could survive a bit longer without supplementation. But information? Not having the right information could mean life or death, right? As she'd told Scottie, they were in uncharted territory. You didn't survive uncharted territory by stumbling around blindly. You did so by collecting as much information as you could. You *charted* that territory.

With that foremost in her mind, she continued down the street with more confidence in her step, her arms swaying back and forth as she hummed quietly to herself. As she walked, she found her troubles falling away, and she started to enjoy the experience. It was honestly a beautiful day. Sun shining, blue skies, not too hot, and a light breeze ruffling her hair and clothing.

It was another half hour before she spotted the Capitol, its distinctive shape standing out just as much as the sudden shock of green surrounding it. But as she approached, slipping between the manicured trees, she paused, realizing she probably wouldn't find answers here as the scene settled into her brain.

Where are the cars?

From here, she could see the green lawn stretching out in front of her, with pathways looping it on either side, and the US Capitol just beyond. Between the lawn and the building, there should have been a small parking lot with cars circling the lawn. She'd once picked Thom up from work here when his car had broken down, so she remembered what it looked like.

Except there was nothing. No cars. No people.

Shouldn't there be… something?

Maybe they had to walk here when the power died.

It was a possibility, but one she was losing faith in as the anxiety started to churn in her gut once more, darkening the previously sunny day in her eyes.

She thought about turning back, about not even trying to find anyone, but there *could* be people inside, and she'd been away for hours. It wouldn't take long to go inside and be sure.

Plus, she was already here. It would be kind of a waste not to at least check it out, right?

Jess started to step out from the line of trees when suddenly, she heard voices. Her first reaction was excitement.

Yes! There's someone here!

She turned toward the noise, her body wanting to run to it in excitement after the letdown of the empty parking lot, but she held herself back.

You don't know who they are.

They might be dangerous.

So, instead, she pressed up harder against the tree, its bark digging into her exposed skin. Their words drifted into her ears, and she frowned when she didn't recognize them. Jess closed her eyes, focusing on what they were saying, but still, it didn't sound familiar, and she definitely knew her way around languages. She wasn't a linguist or anything, but she knew English and Mandarin and was starting to learn Spanish from living with Inez for a while. She could recognize every Romance and Asiatic language, though she often couldn't differentiate them. Same with Germanic languages. She also knew a few words in Usan, though she'd never bothered to learn more than a few greetings; things like, hi, how are you, and do you speak English?

This, however, was like no language she'd ever heard before, and red flags started waving madly in her head. She pressed harder against the tree as she craned her neck around, trying to figure out where the voices were coming from.

Why are they here?

She racked her brain, but couldn't think of a single valid reason someone with *good* intentions would be speaking a language other than English around the Capitol in a time of crisis.

Then she saw them. At first, she didn't quite know what she was seeing. They looked like any other group of soldiers from this distance. They were wearing uniforms and carrying weapons, and she wondered if maybe the Pentagon had sent a team to check on the Capitol after the power had gone out. That would make sense, right?

But then why aren't they speaking English?

And *that* was when she noticed their tails. It was the movement that caught her eye, a hypnotic swaying motion that gently shifted back and forth, feeling at odds with the confident, swift way they crossed the lawn.

But that wasn't the only thing that set them apart. Shortly after the swaying motion of their tails caught her gaze, her brain picked up on their skin. She couldn't see a lot of detail, but she *could* pick up the color well enough against their dark uniforms in the bright sunlight. It was red. They had red skin.

Oh shit!

The fleet.

It invaded.

She spun around, holding her hand against her mouth, afraid to so much as breathe. Her entire body was shaking with fear, and tears welled on her eyelids, threatening to spill over. She was clutching her bow tightly against her chest, afraid her shaking hands would have it banging against the tree behind her and giving her away.

Even through the fog of fear, a small voice in her head was saying, *See? This is why there's been radio silence.* She didn't really want to hear it, didn't even want to think it, but the voice was unassailable.

As she heard the aliens behind her continuing on their journey, her lungs were starting to burn from not getting enough oxygen. Then finally, when their voices grew fainter and fainter, she collapsed against the tree, letting her hand drop, her entire body sagging in exhaustion.

Oh God, that was close.

But then, not even a moment later, two more voices, also completely foreign, spoke up from almost right behind her.

Oh shit, I'm dead.

She held her breath, hoping they hadn't heard her when she'd let her guard down.

Had she made any noises?

Were they even paying attention?

Her muscles ached and a sick feeling started to suffuse her entire body as they slowly followed the others, eventually growing quiet as well.

She was relieved, but also afraid to relax, and slowly peeked out from behind the tree. From here, she could see the group, six in total, moving toward the Capitol building, two lagging behind the others. None of them seemed close enough to hear her, and none of them were looking in her direction. "Oh, God," she said as she turned and dropped her head against the rough bark of the tree that had been her sanctuary. "That was close."

Tired but resigned, she pushed off the tree and looked back at the aliens, ready to go home.

"Fuck. This is not the information I was looking for," she said to herself. She turned, looking back the way she'd come, back toward home.

"What am I gonna tell everyone?"

*V*an looked at him, flabbergasted, as he said the word "mate," like it didn't even compute. Davin felt silly for even speaking it into existence. But with that sweet scent in the air, it was like an ear worm, something you just couldn't resist immersing yourself in. He wanted to follow his nose, to trace her scent, until he could pull her into his arms. It was an addiction that made his brain strain to focus on what was important, the mission.

This is *important!* his mind insisted, trying to draw him back toward thoughts of his absent mate.

He ground his teeth, struggling to keep his frustrations from showing as his instincts warred with his rational mind. *This* was why people took medications to prevent "biological mating," as they called it. It was seen as a curse of their biology, something to be eradicated and suppressed. And yet, while he was in the thick of it, he had a hard time understanding *why* people derided it so. He had a vague impression of being indifferent before, but now he couldn't help relating to Grace's perspective some. The instinctual imperative of mating gave him a degree of certainty he'd never felt before.

After all, when dating, you only *hoped* the two of you would be compatible. With mating, you *knew.*

Still, this was the worst fucking time.

You have a mission. An important one, he reminded himself as he slowly breathed through his mouth, hoping to force the scent from his nose and get his logical brain in control once more.

"Davin?"

"I'll be fine," he said, though he didn't really believe his own words. His body felt on edge, and a deeper, more animalistic part of his psyche kept calling him to succumb like some drumbeat pounding through his skull, egging him on until action was inevitable. "I am fine," he insisted, as much an affirmation to himself as a reassurance to his second in command.

Moments ticked by, but eventually Davin felt steadier, more in control. He started reminding himself *why* he couldn't go after her.

We need to reestablish communication with Earth Command.

We need to figure out what happened here.

We need to help the humans.

Each statement helped center him more and more, and finally, he looked up, realizing the rest of the team were now *far* ahead of them. "We should catch up." He started walking forward once more, tempted to jog, but determined not to make a big deal out of what had just happened. Hopefully, no one would question it. Hopefully, Van would keep his mouth shut.

Like that's ever gonna happen, he scoffed to himself.

Davin smirked. Even *thinking* Van might leave it alone was a pipe dream. Van was many things, but willing to let things go wasn't one of them. It was one of the reasons they were so close. Van was always the first to call him out on his bullshit, which wasn't exactly what you'd expect, considering his demeanor.

It also wasn't something he wanted to deal with right now so, determined to delay the conversation as long as possible, he kept Van at his back while they caught up with the others.

As they finally broke through the tree line, they got their first unobstructed view of the Capitol. From the outside, it was big and ostentatious, but when they *entered*, the interior was even worse. Big spaces, ornate carvings built into the walls, and massive paintings added to the extravagance, which was already over the top. In contrast, the Drakonian "capitol" building was a plain, no-nonsense building that had been added onto so many times, the structure itself was utter chaos to navigate.

Navigating *this* Capitol, by contrast, was fairly simple, and they found themselves in the rotunda in no time at all. As they entered, their steps echoed off the flooring, making him cringe, but in spite of good acoustics, no other sounds were present. He heard no voices, no other steps, no movements or sounds of any kind.

"I don't think anyone's here," Grace said, stating the obvious as she slowly spun in place, occasionally leaning a little to see down a hallway.

"Okay," Davin said, "You know what to do. We're breaking off into pairs. Keep in constant contact and meet back here in the rotunda when you've finished your sweep." With a hand gesture, he dismissed them, but as he took in his surroundings, a churning doubt settled into his gut and somehow he *knew* they wouldn't find anyone here.

Several hours later, they'd finished checking the Capitol building and so called "White House." They hadn't encountered a single soul. It was also clear that the power outage was affecting these essential government buildings, even after all the time that had passed. Either no attempts had been made to restore power, or they'd been unable to do so.

So what does that mean?

He didn't have an answer. As such, once they'd explored the two buildings, they headed back to the shuttle. The entire time, Van eyed him pointedly, but Davin refused to give him an opening to talk.

So instead, he led the team in silence as they returned to the shuttle, everyone far more quiet after their failure to reestablish contact. The first leg of the trip was relatively nice, peaceful even, as they crossed from the White House to the US Capitol. But the moment he approached the trees surrounding the Capitol building, he froze, his senses hijacked once more.

Her scent.

In spite of the hours that had passed, her enticing aroma had yet to fade. It still felt just as strong as before, a kick to the gut that blurred his focus and made him want to follow his nose. He pushed through, hoping it would be easier once he made it past the trees.

It wasn't.

Instead, her scent was slightly stronger, and his resolve weakened with every step forward. As he continued, his movements grew more relaxed, his tension eased, and he found his mind lolling, no longer as aware of his surroundings.

Damn it. This is the path she took, isn't it?

Davin snapped out of it for a moment, knowing that following in her footsteps was a disaster waiting to happen, but this was also the same path they'd planned for returning to the shuttle. He could divert them, but it would add significant time to their trip, and he couldn't give a justification without exposing himself to scrutiny he wasn't prepared for just yet.

So, he suffered in silence. Keeping his mind sharp while her scent constantly teased him required a great but futile effort, causing him to travel down the road on autopilot. It wasn't until he reached the bridge that he finally snapped out of it. His senses sharpened as her scent suddenly intensified, making him realize that her scent *had* faded. The contrast was like night and day, and made him wonder if she was near, or if even *this* intense experience was a washed out copy of the real deal.

As he came to his senses, Van was now ahead of him, his gaze boring into him with that same look of concern from before.

You stopped again.

They were standing in the middle of the road, staring at each other, but while Van seemed very focused on *him*, Davin couldn't say the same in kind. No, his mind only wanted to focus on one thing: *her*. He wanted to know *everything* about her, including where she'd gone. He turned to the side, staring off at a copse of trees that put the smaller one by the Capitol to shame.

What was she doing there?

He wanted to go and see, to find out where she'd gone and why. He wanted to *know*. But he was also torn, because she wasn't in that copse *now*. No, she was up ahead somewhere. She was out of sight and out of touch, and if he ever wanted to find her, he needed to move *forward*.

But I don't want to find her.

Those words felt hollow, like he didn't really believe them. He *needed* to complete the mission. He *needed* to do his job and support his fellow soldiers. But this felt like more than that. It felt like the very air he breathed. He *wanted* the very air he breathed to forever be filled with her sweet scent.

And how stupid is that?

She wasn't even Drakoan. He imagined her running screaming or slamming a door in his face if he told her that her *scent* meant they were destined to be together. Then again, a lot of Drakoans would probably do the same… Being "mates" wasn't exactly a sure thing, especially in modern times.

But try telling his brain that right now.

"Come on," Van said gently, twining their arms together and lightly pulling him forward.

Davin went willingly, hating himself for how he was feeling. He should be leading the team, but *he* was the one being led. He couldn't even control his own actions right now.

"I'll do the report," Van said as he got them moving again.

Davin nodded, and they continued like that until they reached the shuttle.

Van let go, leading the team inside, but Davin couldn't bring himself to follow. The last leg of the trip had taken them farther away from her scent, and he just *knew* that the shuttle, with its life support systems and air filters, would erase the very last traces of her scent. He just couldn't bear it. He *needed* that scent, that connection to her. He couldn't imagine being without it.

So instead, he sat down on the ramp and looked out over the view of Earth he had from this small little corner of the planet. Grasses swayed in the breeze, partially hiding the paths through the park, while trees seemed to pop up randomly, obscuring the view of the surrounding buildings. It was quiet and peaceful, but he felt no peace. The more her scent dissipated, the more agitated he became. Before long, he had to stand, he had to move. He paced behind the shuttle, and when that didn't work, he did circuits around it. No one bothered him, and he couldn't decide if that was better or worse.

How much time has passed?

He knew Van would be reporting back to the fleet, informing them of their status and getting everyone else's statuses as well. He also knew that the moment Van was done, he would come looking for him, looking for answers.

Just thinking about it put Davin even more on edge. All his muscles felt too tense. He tried shaking them out, controlling his breathing, increasing his pace. Nothing helped. His body was telling him to move. His body was telling him to act. And while his mind was clearer now that he was farther away from her scent trail, it didn't bring him comfort. He wanted to dive head first into that fog, embrace it wholeheartedly.

Are you insane?

You have a mission!

He took in another shaky breath, letting it out slowly, hoping to get himself back under control. But he couldn't quite get his mind back on the mission, and he was starting to struggle to remember why it was so damned important in the first place.

He found himself making wider and wider circles around the shuttle, and before he knew it, he stumbled on her scent trail again. It was pure ecstasy, and without conscious thought, he found himself following it as the sun dipped low over the horizon. Like an auspicious omen, the sky before him was starting to warm into colors that reminding him of Drakonian skin tones, bringing a small smile to his face as he walked away, his responsibilities a distant memory.

EPISODE SEVEN

What are We Gonna Do?

*J*ess took far longer than she needed getting back home. She'd spent hours around the Anacostia Riverwalk Trail and had even managed to catch a couple rabbits in the process. Their weight hung heavily, though, in the bag on her back as she approached the front door.

The familiar structure seemed alien and intimidating after everything she'd seen today. She was tempted to just turn around and hope no one had seen her standing on the front lawn like an idiot.

What am I gonna do?

She didn't have an answer, but she couldn't stand here forever. *Eventually*, she would have to go inside and face her friends.

"Aliens have invaded Earth," she said to no one, practicing for the inevitable conversation to follow.

"I saw aliens today. I don't know who's in charge now."

She took slow breaths, hoping to curtail the panic that rose up every time she thought about their new reality. She could feel the pressure building, like the churning waters growing increasingly intense in a wave pool until you felt like you could barely keep yourself from drowning.

The panic starting to grow out of control, she filled her lungs completely in one massive pull of air, then let it out in a slow, audible breath. "You've got this. Just tell them. Don't worry about things you can't control. Don't worry about the future. That will come in time. Worry about the now, the here."

She took another deep breath, letting it out equally slowly.

"What is the here? What is the now?"

The here was home, her and her friends. The here was how they were going to survive and protect themselves. The now was that they were relatively safe. They had food and shelter. The weather was being cooperative. For the time being, they were safe. She'd seen aliens, but they'd been all the way at the Capitol building, *miles* away. She didn't know why they were there, but they weren't *here*, at least not yet.

"Focus on the here and now," she said one last time as she took another deep breath, then started walking toward the house. She pulled her keys from her pocket, unlocking the door as a surreal sense of disconnect washed over her. When she stepped inside, it was to silence.

Are they even here?

Is everyone gone?

She knew immediately it was a ludicrous thought. Jess was the first person to have left since the power went out. Why would any of them have left the property now? "Hello?" she said to the entryway, but no one answered.

Frowning, she moved on, walking into the kitchen, where she shrugged off her bag and placed it on the kitchen table. Then, needing the reassurance that everyone was okay, she stepped up to the sliding glass doors that faced the backyard. When she found everyone dutifully helping with the garden or goofing off, she let out a breath of relief. Jess smiled, grateful for and envious of their blissful innocence.

With a nod, she turned, deciding to give them just a little more time in ignorance. She returned to the kitchen table and pulled out the plastic bag containing her kills. She felt a moment of unease at their dead weight pulling against her grip, at the sight of their diminutive forms through the transparent material. Her gorge rose as she pulled them out and dropped them into the sink. They looked so innocent, like they were only sleeping, and she hated what she would have to do next.

Maybe I can wait. Get someone else to do it.

She shook her head. No. If she was going to hunt, if she was going to kill, then she was going to have to face all the unpleasantness that came along with it.

Besides, was she really willing to put that on her friends?

Turning away so she wouldn't have to face what she was about to do, she focused instead on what she would need. Jess tried to remember her last experience with a dead body, dissecting a cat in her college anatomy labs. She'd used a scalpel then. She didn't have one of those now, but maybe a paring knife would do? With that thought in mind, she wandered to the knife block on the counter and, unfamiliar with the layout, pulled out knife after knife until her hand gripped the one she was looking for. She then opened and closed the cupboards until she found where Amanda kept the cutting boards.

Man, I really don't cook enough, do I?

When she had all her supplies ready, she took the first rabbit from the sink. Staring down at the soft furred creature, her gorge rose once again. At least with the cat, the room had been filled with the intense smell of formaldehyde, the animal had been fairly cold, and she'd been wearing gloves. But as she rested her hand on the animal's flank to hold it steady, she thought she could still feel its body warmth, and her eyes welled with tears. She sniffed once, then got to work, trying to keep her mind blank and breathe carefully through her mouth.

When the fur, the skin, was finally gone, it got easier. She'd bought whole chickens and Cornish hens before, so without all that fur, she could finally see it as just meat, and she calmed down. She moved on to cutting the meat from the bone, much like she would with meat from the grocery store.

But when she finished and stepped back, it didn't look like a lot of food, and her guilt gnawed at her anew.

Why did I do this?

Staring down at the little pile on the cutting board, she felt like a monster, taking two lives for what would probably only be a small supplement to their food reserves.

This is why I never went hunting with my father.

Maybe it would have been different if she'd been able to find a larger animal, maybe a deer. Deer had a *lot* of meat on them. A single deer could probably provide for a few days, maybe more. She wasn't really sure how heavy the average deer was or how much of it would provide usable meat.

But that didn't matter. She *hadn't* found a deer, and there was no point thinking about it. Setting those thoughts aside, she turned to the sink and washed her hands, then walked back to the sliding glass doors. This time, she pushed them open.

"Jess!" Scottie called almost immediately, practically bouncing over to see her. When he reached her, he engulfed her in a hug, using his larger form to lift and swing her back and forth, her toes barely brushing the ground.

"Down, boy," she said, glaring at him playfully.

He put her down as the others started trickling over.

"You're back," Amanda said, smiling as she crossed the yard in her sundress, somehow looking put together and feminine in spite of the almost apocalyptic situation they were coping with.

Before long, everyone else had stopped what they were doing, circling around her curiously.

"Where did you go?"

"What's it like out there?"

"Did you bring anything back?"

Questions came at her rapid fire, surprising her as she hadn't thought anyone but Scottie had noticed her absence. She glared over at him, but he was looking away, trying to act innocent and failing miserably.

She turned back to Amanda. "There's some rabbit on the counter. It's ready to cook."

"Oh. I've never cooked rabbit before. Interesting." She was off immediately, the door thunking closed behind her, leaving Jess at the mercy of the rest of her friends.

"So… what did you find?" Thom asked, looking ridiculous in a button up dress shirt with the sleeves rolled to his elbows. His hands were coated in dirt from helping in the garden, and even though his pants were black, she could still see the faint stains from kneeling on the ground.

Do I tell them?

Jess looked around at the expectant faces, wishing someone would tell her what to do. She turned around, watching through the glass as Amanda approached the counter with the rabbit meat on it, completely oblivious to the bomb Jess was about to drop.

"Well?" Melissa said, her voice sharp as a knife.

Jess sighed, bracing herself for the inevitable as she turned back around and forced herself to make eye contact.

What do I say?

Her friends were leaning toward her, eager to hear about the outside world, completely starved for information after the days-long communication blackout. She swallowed heavily, then tried to square her shoulders. As she finally looked up, meeting each person eye to eye, she stopped on Scottie, who was looking at her with compassion in his gaze, like he *knew.* He couldn't know. There was no way he could *possibly* know, but his eyes said otherwise.

"I… well… there wasn't really anyone out on the streets." *Thankfully.* "I took the Sousa Bridge. Headed over to the Capitol." She paused, remembering the empty parking lot, remembering the alien voices and red skin, remembering the paralyzing fear that seemed almost too intense to have happened hours before. She took a careful breath in and out, not wanting to show what she was feeling, and continued. "The parking lot was empty."

There were aliens.

"Well, that makes sense," Thom said, crossing his arms and smearing brown stains on his pristine white shirt without seeming to notice.

Jess stared, remembering all the times Thom had balked at even the idea of leaving the house without being perfectly pressed. Her gaze was stuck on those streaks of brown, but he didn't even squirm at her uninterrupted focus. He showed no discomfort whatsoever, his facade immaculate, but the defensive posture and seeming obliviousness to the state of his clothes spoke otherwise.

"Come on, now, Thom, don't be a fucking idiot." Melissa dismissed him as she turned, zeroing in on Jess, her eyes gleaming with an uncomfortable intensity. "Did you go inside? Was there anyone there? Did you find anything?" With each question, her body grew more tense, her words faster, her focus absolute.

Again, Jess thought of the aliens crossing the lawn and shook her head. No, she hadn't gone inside. She'd been too afraid to. That was the direction the *aliens* were heading.

"Now, Melissa. Cálmate." Inez stepped forward, putting a reassuring hand on Melissa's shoulder.

Melissa rolled her eyes, but she also ceded to her friend's words. Inez had that kind of power over Melissa, being the only one in the house capable of settling her when she was on a tear.

"Well, what *did* you find?" Scottie said.

"Aliens." It was the only thing she *could* say. The only word that would escape her locked vocal cords when she thought of that moment.

"What?!" Melissa shouted.

"She said 'aliens,' bitch," Scottie quipped, teasing her.

"Oh, shut up."

Scottie snort-laughed, then looked over at Jess, a smirk on his face. It was clearly a struggle as he tried to get serious. "Okay." He clapped his hands together. "What about the aliens? How many were there? What did they look like? Did they look dangerous?"

"I..." She looked around her, heart lodged in her throat, unsure where to start. "They looked military." She racked her brain. What else? Her heart raced like a hummingbird's wings as she continued spewing the first thing to come to mind, the lock on her words finally broken. "There were six of them. And they had red skin and tails."

Scottie started rubbing his chin thoughtfully, giving her a reprieve when he started talking. "Hm. Red skin and tails... Are you sure it was skin? Could it have been scales?"

Jess froze, remembering the terror before her mind could process the rest of the memory. The fear felt like a warning sign telling her not to enter, but this wasn't something she could escape. So far, she'd only remembered those moments when they'd flashed through her brain unbidden, but now she had no choice. Her only option was to face them head on. She clenched her fists as she forced herself to remember more details. The voices came to her first, the strangeness of them her first clue that something was terribly wrong. Then it was the hypnotic sway of their tails, the black on red, but no matter how much she tried, she couldn't make out any more detail. She couldn't tell if they'd had scales.

She shook her head, frustrated that she didn't know. It was just one detail, but it was so very fucking important. That detail could mean the difference between ally and enemy, friend and foe. She wanted to scream, but instead she just deflated, saying, "I don't know."

It felt like a failure, a defeat, like she'd let her friends down, but Scottie only shrugged, letting her off the hook far too easily. "Could be Drakoans."

"They're allies," Thom said, arms still crossed.

"Allies can still stab us in the back," Melissa sniped sarcastically.

"They might not have done that," Jess said, surprising herself. After all, the first thing she'd thought when she'd seen the aliens was that Earth had been invaded, but maybe this was a good thing? Maybe they were here to help? It hadn't occurred to her that they might have been good guys when she first saw them. After all, they'd been living under the threat of a potential alien invasion. What else was she supposed to think?

"She's right." Scottie nodded, giving Jess a gentle smile of encouragement. "If they *were* Drakoan, they might have been there at the behest of the government or military or something." He shrugged.

"But what if they aren't the Drakoans?" Inez said, her voice even quieter than usual. "What if the fleet failed? What if we've already been invaded?"

"Then we do the best we can." Jess tried to sound confident, imagining how Melissa would be in her position. Her voice would be strong, maybe flippant or sarcastic. Her chin would be high, her shoulders back. She might even have a hand on her hip, showing just a bit of the attitude she was known for.

Meanwhile, the real Melissa wrapped an arm around Inez's shoulder, pulling her close to her side. "Come on. Let's go inside and see if we can help with dinner."

Inez nodded, and they walked away.

Thom nodded as well, finally lowering his arms. "No point worrying about it now," he said before he followed them inside.

That left just her and Scottie. She looked over at him, feeling the full weight of the unknown looming before her. "What are we gonna do?"

He scoffed, shaking his head. "Don't ask me. I'm just a Trekkie."

After dinner, they settled in the living room, each of them holding their stomachs as they groaned over how full they were. Jess felt ridiculous as she recalled thinking that the two rabbits would only be a small supplement to their diet. Now, she suspected her guilt had twisted her perceptions, leaving her unable to see the truth. Not only had Amanda made a fairly big meal, the biggest they'd had in days, but she'd asked Thom to put the rest in the smoker out back. "Usually, I wouldn't suggest running the smoker for only a few pounds of meat, but I can't see wasting it," Amanda had said. So they'd ended up eating on the back patio with the rich scent of smoking meat filling their nostrils, enhancing their meal and reassuring them that there was still more to come.

Maybe because of that, the mood in the room was better than it had been in days. They all felt more secure, hopeful, and happy, and as they relaxed into their seat cushions, the conversation naturally transitioned to the aliens she'd seen earlier. This time, Amanda was the most engaged initially, making up for having been absent for the first conversation. Before long, the lassitude caused by the meal evaporated, each of her friends sitting on the edges of their seats as they debated the significance of the alien presence.

Jess understood why they were so obsessed, but also, she just wanted a break. She wanted to talk about stupid shit like Dungeons & Dragons or the latest Sci-Fi movie or show. She wanted to listen as Scottie enthused about the game he was playing or Amanda chattered excitedly about a recipe she couldn't wait to try. What she wouldn't give for just a little slice of normalcy right now!

But as that wasn't possible, and the conversation continued to obsessively spiral around the aliens, she stood up and paced to the window. She looked out at the sky over the houses across the street, calmed slightly by the stunning array of colors painting the day's end. She leaned against the window, which was surprisingly cool against her shoulder, and tried to tune out the voices of her friends.

She couldn't really blame them for their interest. Not only was it a subject that affected them all greatly, but it was a mystery, and while trapped in their own home without internet, it wasn't like there was much else to talk about.

But *they* weren't there. They didn't have to see the aliens in person, didn't have to feel the adrenaline and fear that came along for the ride. After the day she'd had, she was completely exhausted and just needed a break from it all.

She sighed as she continued to stare out the window. There wasn't even anything to look at. All their neighbors were inside, no cars were going down the street, no animals were being walked, no children were playing. From this vantage point, it was easy to imagine that the world had already ended, that humans were gone and only their constructions were left to speak of their existence.

So, at first, what caught her attention was simply *movement*. Since everything was so still, *any* movement was noticeable.

But since it was at the very edge of her view through the window and partially obscured by trees and bushes, that was all she could see.

She craned her neck, leaning harder against the glass. In her mind, she imagined the pane giving way and spilling her out onto the bushes below. She looked away and smiled, but then focused back on the place where she'd spotted movement.

What was it?

Was it just a neighbor outside?

Could it be the government finally trying to make some sort of contact with its citizens?

The next thing she noticed was dark clothing. It blended well with the deep green of the vegetation, noticeable but not stark. As she continued to watch, she started to draw conclusions. It was definitely a person. They were alone. They were walking somewhere. For several minutes, she couldn't see much more than that. The mature neighborhood had equally mature trees with thick, low-hanging branches. From outside, she probably could have seen more, but from here? There were just too many obstacles.

Several more minutes passed as she curiously but idly watched the person travel through the neighborhood, inexorably moving in her direction. She had no idea where the person was going, but she was now invested in finding out.

Who were they?

What did they look like?

Where were they going?

She couldn't even *hear* the conversation going on behind her at this point. It wasn't even background noise. She wasn't even sure if they were still in the room with her.

And she didn't care.

Then she finally got a real glimpse of the person. It happened in stages, her nose now cartoonishly plastered to the window. At first, she could see their form unobstructed, but they were cast in shadow. All she could tell was that they looked big in comparison to the bushes behind them. Then they started walking out into the late evening sun, revealing a mouthwateringly powerful build in a dark outfit. In her boredom, she fantasized about running her hands over those muscles, maybe even untucking that shirt and sneaking her hands up underneath it. She wondered what he would do if she changed course, instead reaching into those surprisingly tight pants. Would he groan? Gasp? Stop her?

What are you doing?

She pulled back, a little disgusted with herself for mind fucking the poor bastard.

Not cool, Jess. Not cool.

Shaking herself, she focused back on the guy, but this time paying attention to the mysteries he still had, like his currently shadowed face.

Wish I had binoculars.

It was easy enough to see his big, well-defined muscles from this distance, but his facial features were a lot smaller and thus a lot harder to discern. Was he handsome? Cute? Boyish?

Why am I doing this?

Am I really this bored?

Still, he was a mystery, a mystery that had nothing to do with the threat looming over their heads, and she eagerly awaited the unveiling of the answer, happily devouring any distraction she could lay her hands on. She held her breath as the line of shadow crept higher and higher, on the brink of revealing him fully.

She frowned when sunlight finally touched skin. Was he sunburned? Was the sunset creating an optical illusion? The line of shadow continued to move upward, revealing surprisingly red skin, leaving her with a new mystery to solve.

Why was he so red?

When it exposed his mouth, it didn't look like he was in discomfort, so she nixed sunburn as a potential cause.

As she continued to watch, a sinking dread started to settle in her stomach. He was growing closer, and his skin was just too red, too vibrant, to be the result of the warm light from the setting sun.

He stepped out onto the street, now only a house or two down the road, and the air froze in her lungs as recognition finally clicked in her brain, and the mystery was solved.

It's him.

Memories of the encounter this afternoon flashed through her brain. Red skin. Black uniforms. Swishing tails. Foreign words.

Paralyzing fear.

Her lungs started to complain, the pressure building as she continued to stand there, staring at the impossibility before her.

It can't be.

But it was. The proof was right before her, walking toward her one step at a time. Her hands felt cold against the glass, her fingers reflexively gripping the slick material. She finally sucked in a breath, and it was like the world had suddenly started up again.

He followed me home.

She stepped back from the window, panic flooding her as the paralysis ended.

He followed me home.

"Jess?" someone said, but in her current state of mind, she couldn't tell who'd spoken.

She continued backing up, unable to take her eyes off the approaching form. Her legs banged into the coffee table, and she stalled, taking a moment to keep her balance.

Then he turned slightly, and their eyes met through the glass.

He sees me.

He knows where I am.

Then a smirk lifted his lips, and the fear took control.

She screamed.

EPISODE NINE

The Chase Begins

"*J*ess? What's wrong?"

She heard the words, but for the life of her, she still couldn't tell who had spoken them. Her ears were ringing with her own scream and the pounding of her heart in her chest. He was staring at her through the window, and she couldn't take her eyes off him.

How can he be here?

How did he find me?

But those questions were irrelevant. What was more important was that he *had* found her. He was *here*. And she still didn't know if he was a good guy or a bad guy.

Considering he followed me back home, I'm leaning toward bad guy.

"Jess?" Someone touched her shoulder, and she jumped.

"Sorry," she said, finally looking away and over at Amanda, who was staring at her with concern in her eyes. Jess turned back to the window, and her heart lurched in her chest. He was gone. She jerked forward, Amanda's hand slipping from her shoulder, and scoured the scene for any trace of him, but her view from the window was still and quiet, not a person in sight.

Did I imagine it?

"Jess?"

She opened her mouth, her first impulse being to tell the truth, but what was the truth? She snapped it closed again, starting to question her own sanity a little.

No one else has seen them.

The panic and urgency she'd been feeling slowly drained out of her as the moments ticked by. She gave the vista one final peruse, not sure if she hoped she would see him or *not* see him.

Am I losing my mind?

She didn't *think* she was. But could you *ever* be certain?

Jess turned away from the window, taking in the expressions of concern on her friends' faces. In that moment, she *knew* she couldn't tell them what she'd seen. So instead, she shrugged, trying to smile and laugh it off. "I guess I'm just a little jumpy."

Amanda leaned in, wrapping her arms around her and hugging her, then rocking her back and forth as she always seemed to do. "It's okay. We've got you. Nothing bad's gonna happen, no matter *how* scary it is outside. Anything could happen…"

Yeah, like an alien following you home.

She didn't say that, though.

Amanda leaned back. "…but *here*, you're safe." She smiled.

Jess wanted to contradict her, but she also didn't want to scare her friends, especially if it really *had* been a figment of her imagination. So instead, she said, "I just need some time to myself." She shrugged out of Amanda's hold, then looked around her. "See you guys in the morning?"

Amanda nodded, a fragile smile on her face as Jess turned away, intending to go up to her room.

But she stopped at the bottom of the stairs, a thought occurring to her.

A lot of the windows are open.

Even the ones that were closed weren't exactly military grade. *She* could break one with very little effort. If that alien *hadn't* been her imagination, the house was no protection at all. For a brief moment, the fear from earlier returned. She reached out, gripping the stair railing. The smooth wood pressed hard into the flesh of her hand as she became lightheaded, her vision narrowing alarmingly.

She reached out, slamming a hand into the wall. "Stop this," she whispered to herself, taking in a ragged breath. She pressed harder, trying to feel in control again through sheer force of will. "This is not helping," she said under her breath. "This type of fear helps no one. Face your fears." She took in and let out another deep breath. "What am I so afraid of?"

Her mind went blank, and she realized she didn't have an answer.

My God, am I just freaking myself out over nothing?

With that thought, the tension in her body suddenly dissolved. Her jaw relaxed, and she let go of the railing and wall. She stood up straight once more, looking around her like she didn't even recognize her surroundings. "Why am I afraid?" she whispered.

Why was seeing an alien scary? When she thought back on it, she realized none of the aliens had been terribly threatening. They'd *looked* military, but while they'd been carrying weapons, they'd held those weapons with lax grips, like they weren't expecting a fight.

And more recently, the one staring in at her hadn't even been *holding* a weapon. His hands had been empty.

Truth be told, *none* of them had made any threatening gestures toward her, even when they knew she was there.

She turned, leaning against the wall as she thought some more, her brow furrowing.

They could still be the bad aliens. She couldn't dismiss that possibility, but if they were, why had that one shown up here? Why was he alone? If he had nefarious intentions, why did he just stand there?

She didn't have any answers, but did that really matter? In the grand scheme of things, no one was ever truly safe. You could drop dead of an aneurism, never knowing it was even a risk. You could get hit by a car or die from something falling off a skyscraper and onto your head. You could never anticipate *all* the dangers in life. You could just try to be as careful as possible while also living your life with confidence. In fact, sometimes that very confidence was what kept you safe. After all, bad guys often chose their victims carefully. They were far more likely to choose someone skittish over someone confidently taking up space.

With that in mind, she pushed off the wall and changed directions, passing through the kitchen and on to the sliding glass doors. She stared out into the growing dimness, seeing no one and nothing in the familiar space.

Prove it to yourself, Jess.

Prove you're not afraid.

Jess took in one final slow, deep breath, then carefully pushed the door aside, mindful that if she didn't do it just right, it would jam in its track. She stood there for a moment, a light breeze touching her face while insects chirped before her and her friends' constant voices hummed behind her. If she were letting fear get to her, she *could* have been alarmed by the shadowy corners, imagining all the things they could conceal. She *could* obsess over the sections of the house's back wall currently hidden from her view, places where an alien could easily hide, invisible until it was too late.

She forced a laugh past her vocal cords, determined to make light of those imaginings.

No one's in the backyard, Jess.

Don't be silly.

Prove you're not afraid.

You've got this.

She stepped out onto the uneven pavers, then turned to close the door behind her, determined not to be a chicken by giving herself an easy way out. Even if the alien had been outside the window, what were the chances that he'd not only stuck around, but that he'd snuck into their backyard like a pervert? That was just silly. He was clearly a soldier. That was the type of antics teenagers got up to, not fully grown adults.

She continued forward, passing the picnic table where they'd eaten dinner and the smoker, which was still belching sweet-smelling aromas into the air. The pavers quickly ended, and she stepped onto the grass, which was showing some yellow spots where it had not received enough water lately.

Jess looked down at the grass. Then on an impulse, she kicked off her shoes, savoring the feel of the cool blades on her bare soles, letting it ground her in the moment. She imagined her fear slowly oozing down her body, down her legs, into her feet, then out into the soil. She sighed as the weight of it seemed to evaporate, making her feel like herself for the first time in hours.

With a smile and a new lightness to her step, she set her sights on a patio chair on the other side of the yard. She crossed the intervening distance with rapid strides, then settled into the chair and leaned back, enjoying the way the last rays of daylight silhouetted the house's outline before her. For the first time in days, she honestly felt like maybe everything would turn out all right. This wasn't just empty reassurances like she'd been giving her friends. No, she truly *felt* this. A calm settled over her.

She laughed. "Damn, why don't I do this more often?"

Her career involved spending long stretches of time indoors, and it was pretty common for her to lose track of time. She would often look up to find that night had settled in around her while she wasn't looking. She kept telling herself she would spend more time outside, that she would go for walks, spend time at the park, or sit out here with her friends, but it was just so easy to let time slip away from her, especially when she was most productive in the mornings and afternoons.

But here? In this chair? Sure, time was slipping away, but she didn't care. In fact, the longer she sat there, the more her body seemed to melt into the chair and the more she forgot about why she'd been so stressed in the first place. The color slowly leeched from the sky and darkness settled in, but she was still hesitant to go inside. She watched the house as candles were lit and her friends wandered off to their beds. Meanwhile, crickets and other night creatures started serenading her in earnest, their voices swelling into an orchestra around her. She was tempted to sit out here until the mosquitos invariably ate her alive.

But it wasn't the mosquitos that ended up disturbing her peace. It was a noise, both subtle and impossible to define. It shattered the stillness of the night like someone kicking over a metal trashcan. She tensed, and even the insects grew silent in the wake of it.

"Hello?" she said, sitting up straighter in her chair. The darkness had closed in around her. At some point, all the candles had been snuffed out inside the house, leaving only the moon and stars to illuminate her surroundings, neither of which was doing a terribly good job.

She waited, simultaneously hoping someone would answer and that *no one* would. Her mind drifted to the alien man she'd seen out front what felt like hours ago. Could he still be around? Had he been waiting for the perfect opportunity?

No.

She shook her head, frowning at her own silliness. Why would he have waited so long? Night had settled in quite a while ago, and she'd been sitting on this chair alone for even longer. If he'd had nefarious plans, he could have enacted them at any time. Her friends had been at the front of the house. They probably wouldn't have heard a struggle.

Reassured by her reasoning, she began to settle back into her chair, still alert but starting to believe it had just been an animal. More than a couple of their neighbors had large dogs. A Great Dane, a lab, she thought there was even a husky down the street. Any one of them could have been let out into their own backyard for one final romp before bedtime. Maybe the sound had carried through the night air in a way she wasn't used to. After all, she didn't *usually* sit out in the dark.

As she let herself believe, her back unfurled, her shoulders gradually settling against the chair once more. Like a blanket settling over the night, the insects resumed their songs, the sound filling the air, and a yappy dog started barking in the distance. Everything felt so *normal* that it was hard to believe she was living through a global crisis.

But even with all her assurances, even with how *normal* every-thing felt, she just couldn't settle into the peace she'd found before. She was now uncomfortably aware of every shadow and the dangers that could lurk within them.

Would it get darker? She looked up and around her. She could still see fairly well and didn't think she would have trouble getting to the back door, but how long would that last? Was it already as dark as the night would get? Or would she soon find herself stumbling blindly as she tried to reach the house?

I should go inside.

Jess stood up. Her friends were already in bed, and they would probably be up banging around at the crack of dawn. She didn't relish the idea of trying to sleep through that. She missed the days when they used to stay up until all hours playing games or chatting, but without electricity, there just wasn't much to do once the sun set.

With a sigh, she bemoaned how things had changed as she took her first step, but then froze when the shadows to her left shifted, drawing her gaze. She didn't move her head. Instead, like a startled animal, she focused on what she could see from the corners of her vision. She saw nothing at first.

I'm not afraid, she reminded herself. She *knew* that shadows could play tricks on her, that it was probably nothing but a bird or squirrel ruffling branches. She watched, waiting for some telltale sign, a reassurance that all was well. As she waited, she became keenly aware of just how far away the back door was. She wasn't exactly a runner, and if that shadowy form *was* dangerous, she didn't think she could make the door before it got to her.

Jess started moving again, her steps slow and steady as she kept her gaze on the potential threat posed by the shadowy movement. The longer she watched, the more her eyes adjusted. Gradually, she registered more detail. The outline of branches and leaves. The edges of the wooden fence. An empty pot laying on its side.

And something else, something that felt out of place, but didn't at first have an assigned identity in her mind. It was the graceful curves that caught her attention. Too thick and smooth to be that of a tree and too big to be anything else from that end of the yard. It was silhouetted against the fence, eerily ominous in spite of its stillness.

But whatever it was, it was dark, blending partially into the shadows.

Feeling an urgent impulse to get inside, she picked up her pace. Her heart had got the message as well, now racing in her chest like George of the Jungle cranked up on java, making her feel on edge. But her brain still hadn't put the pieces together yet.

Then she spotted that final piece. She noticed something swaying back and forth closer to the ground, like a low-hanging branch swaying in the breeze, and she froze one last time. She knew that movement. She'd *seen* that movement before.

It's him!

She took off at a dead run, racing for the back door. Her footing was unsteady as she reached the pavers, but she barely let that slow her down, her focus completely on the closed doors between her and "safety."

A loud, sharp crack of noise disturbed the silence behind her. She flinched, then slammed up against the glass.

"Wait!" someone said, their deep voice far too close for comfort.

She scrambled for the door handle, but her panic was making her hands shake, and she couldn't get a good grip.

"Stop, please."

She ignored the words, instead yanking on the handle the moment her fingers finally curled around it, but it didn't budge, instead rocking back and forth in its frame.

Shit. I forgot.

She tried again, but finesse was outside of her skill set at the moment, and it rocked again but didn't open. "Damn it!" She turned around. He was practically right behind her, his form looming impossibly large and backlit by the moon, so she could see nothing but his shadowed outline.

Her entire body ran cold, and for a moment, she could barely breathe. She pressed back against the smooth glass of the sliding door, her hand losing its grip on the handle.

What do I do?

He was too close. There was no way she could get inside before he was on her.

Her mind scrambled for options. The front door? Probably locked. An open window? He would just follow her. No phones, so no calling the police. None of her friends had any self defense or martial arts training. Hell, the bulkiest of them was probably Scottie, and he wouldn't harm a fly.

I'm fucked.

No, think, damn it. There has to be something.

Then she remembered. One of her neighbors was a cop. She'd never met them, but she remembered seeing the patrol car in their front drive from time to time. It was the corner lot, and so far away that she couldn't for the life of her imagine reaching it before she was caught, but it was her only chance.

Fuck it.

She pushed off from the door, racing off the patio and into the night.

You'll never make it.

She tried to push that voice out of her mind, but when she passed the corner of the house, she heard a large form barreling after her and all hope fled her.

I'm not gonna make it.

EPISODE TEN

Caught

*J*ess could barely gulp down enough air. She was pumping her limbs as fast as they would go, her entire focus on getting to the neighbor's house.

She felt like she was making no progress at all, like she was standing still.

Her mind popped to those dreams she used to have, where no matter how hard she tried to run, it was like she was trudging through quicksand. *This* felt like that dream, only *this* was real.

And he was getting closer. She could hear him, his heavy footfalls pounding the earth, his breaths puffing into the air behind her.

Jess pushed herself harder, desperate to get a little distance between them, but she might as well have been moving backwards. It took forever to pass by the air conditioner, the trash cans, and finally the garden hose spilling out over the grass in coils. Each item seemed so close, but took so long to reach. Then excitement hit her as she approached the corner of the house, even though it was nowhere near her destination.

Maybe someone will see me.

But the hope was short-lived. The moment she reached the corner, a thick arm looped around her, pulling her off her feet. Her legs flailed and she screamed, beating against him in any way she could. The muscles of his forearm pressed hard against her ribcage, making every breath a battle, especially after running for her life. She pulled and clawed at the flesh there, not even registering its texture, just desperate for escape.

Her ears rang as she struggled fruitlessly against his superior strength. She screamed again, hoping someone would hear. Or, if nothing else, that he had sensitive ears. There was a certain warm glee that filled her at the thought that her screams might hurt him. At this point, she would hurt him any way she could, even if it was only with sound.

But she couldn't fight against him forever. He was strong, and she was *not*. Little by little, weariness settled into her body, and eventually, she just couldn't maintain her outrage. Resignation fell upon her like a weighted blanket, snuffing out any remaining hope of escape. Jess still definitely had adrenaline rushing through her system, but she could already feel the shakiness as it started to wear off.

I'm no match for him.

Her face heated, and she held back an urge to cry in frustration. Jess thought of all the times she'd attended martial arts classes, of all the drills she'd participated in, but that had been years ago, hadn't it? She'd half-heartedly kept up her practice in college, but after? She'd let herself go, falling into a routine where she spent most of her time sitting in front of a computer or a camera.

What's he gonna do to me? she wondered as she squirmed in his arms, trying to make at least *some* room for herself.

Think, Jess. There's got to be something *you can do.*

She'd learned plenty of maneuvers over the years, but with her feet in the air and his arm locked around her torso, she didn't have the leverage or space to perform *any* of them.

And *that* was when she started to notice things.

Humid puffs of air against the back of her neck.

A gentle voice.

A soothing caress.

The tension finally drained from her body as she noticed one last detail: scales. There were scales under her fingertips. She looked down, taking in the red texture covering his muscles. In the dark, the color looked more burgundy, but she ran a tentative finger over it, feeling the edge of each scale.

"I'm not gonna hurt you," he said into her ear, his voice both deep and smooth, soothing now that she was actually paying attention.

It was the first thing he'd said that she'd actually understood, though she realized belatedly that it wasn't the first time he'd spoken in English. *Now*, she remembered hearing someone asking her to wait, to stop. It was the same voice, *his* voice. She stopped struggling, and after several tense moments, he lowered her feet to the ground, but his arm around her middle didn't budge. Neither did the hand that was slowly caressing her, gently running over her head, down her neck, down her arm, then back again.

He's trying to soothe me.

She froze in shock and suddenly all of their encounters took on an entirely different feel. At the Capitol, he'd most likely only been doing his job. As best she could tell, he hadn't even noticed her. And had he come looking for her, or was him standing outside her house a coincidence? Had he simply been surprised to see someone looking through the window?

Or had he seen her at the Capitol, then recognized her through the window, causing him to pause?

But then why wait around? The tension that had left her body only moments before began to rise up again, because she didn't have an answer to that. She could explain away him rushing after her. Maybe he'd wanted to explain himself, or maybe he'd worried she would get lost in the dark. But she couldn't explain him lurking in the shadows for God only knew how long.

And why the hell is he sniffing me?

He was still whispering soothing words in her ear, but now she realized he'd interspersed those words with brief inhales through his nose, which was pressed against her neck. The first time she noticed, it was so short, barely a moment, and she wondered if she'd imagined it, but then he did it again. Leaned in, sniffed, pulled back slightly, then more reassuring words.

Is it an alien thing?

She racked her brain, but she couldn't remember a damned thing about his species off the top of her head. They'd been allies with humans for longer than she'd been alive, but she couldn't say she'd ever really paid much attention when they'd discussed them in class. It had only been a brief chapter, going over the Drakoans and the human colony on Koa, then they'd moved on to other topics.

Maybe sniffing was somehow important to his people? Dogs greeted each other by sniffing each other's butts. Could Drakoans be similar? How was she to know if they had unusual greeting customs? Shrugging and turning her head to the side slightly, she leaned in and sniffed, and her knees instantly went weak as warmth rushed through her.

Holy shit.

He smelled fantastic. She couldn't describe it, really, but he smelled… warm, soothing, like home somehow. It felt like coming home. She had a fleeting impulse to turn around in his arms and cling to him, to feel him up and press her nose against his neck, sucking in as much of that scent as she possibly could. But his grip was like iron, and even taking a deep breath had her battling against his hold. There was no way she was turning around any time soon.

Then he growled, and her legs really *did* give out on her this time. Another warm swell ran through her, this time settling between her legs.

Holy shit, I'm turned on.

She wanted to freeze, to take a step back, but her body felt like cooked noodles, and she was suddenly very keenly aware of every inch of flesh that was pressed against him. She arched, curling backward until her cheek rubbed up against his neck, and she couldn't help pressing her nose against it one more time as she moaned.

A very dim, barely audible voice in the back of her head was wondering what the hell she was doing, what the hell had happened to her, but she quickly pushed it aside in favor of *feeling*. *Feeling* the slight texture of his scaled forearms. *Feeling* the hardness of his muscles against her back. *Feeling* the dampness of his breath. *Feeling* the heat surging inside her.

Then finally, *feeling* something long and hard against her ass.

She stopped her squirming for only a brief moment, taking in the sensation, knowing all too well what it meant.

I should be afraid.

The thought came out of nowhere, but it shouldn't have felt so out of context, so alien. He was a stranger, after all. And they'd never talked, never discussed birth control or STDs.

Hell, he'd been creeping around her backyard, for crying out loud!

I should be running.

I should be screaming.

But instead, she found herself panting for breath, her focus now on her new discovery, and she couldn't help pressing harder against it. What would it look like? What would it *feel* like? Suddenly, she needed to know. She was desperate to know. Jess imagined him slowly divesting her of her clothing, running those strong hands over every inch of skin he exposed. She imagined him reaching one hand between her legs, amping her up with a strong steady finger as his other hand gently caressed her breast and his teeth nipped at her ear. She imagined that growl, him working his pants down, then…

"Please…" she moaned, desperately needing this new fantasy to become a reality.

Davin couldn't think straight, not with her scent filling his nose, her warmth settling into his bones, and her curves pressing into his flesh. It also didn't help that all his blood flow had rushed south, abandoning his brain like it was escaping a sinking ship.

He couldn't blame it, though. His brain was pretty worthless at the moment. All he could think about was the fact that he'd found her. She was *here*, in his arms. He couldn't help leaning in and pressing his nose to her neck once more, breathing in that intoxicating scent like it was the only thing connecting him to sanity. He growled in pleasure, and a new scent perfumed the air. Something even sweeter, more enticing.

Now, the hand that had been trying to soothe her only moments before took on a new intention. His path slowed, and he became even more aware of his senses. The silky smoothness of her skin. The way her chest pressed against his forearm where he held her. The way she shivered when the back of his fingers brushed against the side of her breast. He repeated the gesture, then leaned in and growled right against her ear, hoping to get a repeat of that delicious scent.

He wasn't disappointed. She whimpered, any fight that remained leaving her body for good.

A small smile crossed his face, a little bit of fang peaking out over his lip, pressing into the flesh there in an appealing way. He relaxed his grip around her torso, confident she wouldn't try to escape, and started experimenting with his touch, searching for the best ways to ripen her scent. His hand roamed gently, barely touching as he explored. Her clothing was soft and lightweight, barring him access to her skin, but not obscuring the feel of the curves underneath.

In that moment, he couldn't remember the last time he'd had a woman in his arms, couldn't even remember the best way to please one, but it didn't matter. His mind might be blank, but his instincts were revving into high gear. The more her scent saturated the air, the less he thought and the more he grew frustrated with *anything* getting between him and his prize.

Soon, gentle touches weren't enough. He growled, this time in frustration, and she moaned and collapsed to the ground on all fours, like an offering he couldn't refuse. He started yanking at his clothes, frustrated with each fastener in his way. Her cheek was to the grass, rubbing against it in her desperation to be touched. Meanwhile, her ass pushed up into the air, taunting him with everything he craved.

Cool air touched his scales, and he dropped to his knees behind her, his mind momentarily hijacked by the uncontrollable impulse to reach out and clasp that beautiful behind. Her pants did almost nothing to disguise the ass that waited beneath them, and the heat of her radiated through the stretchy fabric, beckoning him to get on with it.

He rubbed once, twice, and she moaned again, so he grabbed the waistband and yanked, pulling them down to her knees. Her undergarment went with them, exposing two pale, beautiful orbs that looked pristinely white in the moonlight. He reached out, squeezing the flesh there. A shuddering breath left him, and he pulled them apart, exposing her cleft and the glittering flesh that lay farther down. A fresh whiff of her scent hit him, drawing him in like iron to a magnet.

He leaned in, inhaling deeply, and moaned, then pressed his face to her wetness, loving the way she squirmed as he rubbed against her, soaking himself in her essence.

At one point, she gasped, and he pulled back.

"No," she moaned in protest, dragging out the sound.

No more willing to stop than she was, he reached down, tentatively exploring her folds until he found a spot that had her pressing hard against his hand. He touched and circled it experimentally, and she grew urgent with her need, her scent growing even more intense.

She likes this.

He smiled, his fang making another appearance, and he worked that little spot harder, holding his other hand against her hip to keep her right where he wanted her. He watched as she squirmed and begged wordlessly, her entire body animated with need.

His own need pressed hard against his lower abdomen, determined not to be ignored. He shivered as the cool air irritated the flesh there when all he *really* wanted was to feel heat.

Her heat.

He worked her harder, determination filling him as his body grew tight right alongside hers. He *needed* to see her climax, but he wasn't sure how much longer he could keep this up. His mind was screaming at him from all directions. He needed to hold her still. He needed to see her fall apart. He needed to have her. Every urge warred against the next, leaving him panting and begging for an outlet.

Then she broke. Abruptly, her voice was locked inside her, unable to escape. Her head fell back, hair falling along the curve of her bowed spine, further presenting her rear for his use. And against his fingers, he could feel something twitching, much like his own cock twitched when he came, and he smiled.

But the moment of pride was short-lived. The delay had cost him, his own restraint fraying until it finally snapped. He dove forward, his arms caging her in. He pressed his nose to her neck, once again breathing in that impossible scent, then he shifted, pressing his teeth against her neck this time, biting down, but not breaking the skin. She froze, but then she pressed up against his chest, her ass rubbing against him and fraying his nerves even further. He moaned, and he rubbed against her once, twice, then unable to take it anymore, he reached down and lined them up, jerking forward with a single thrust that seated him fully. She gasped, but he held onto her neck, held onto *her*, as he lost himself to her heat. He growled again. He couldn't help himself. It was too much. He was filled with her, and nothing about the next few moments was under his conscious control.

He started moving, filling her again and again as a part of him strained for something his fried brain simply couldn't comprehend. She was gasping, panting, but that wasn't enough for him. He changed his angle, and she moaned. The sound was long, drawn out, and it filled him with satisfaction. He slowed down, focusing on that new angle until he'd mastered it. Then he picked up the pace, hitting her with it again and again until she could barely let out more than a squeak through her poor, abused vocal cords.

Satisfaction filled him, warming him from the inside out, and his entire body felt on fire, but like before, it was paired with a determination that wouldn't let up. He *couldn't* give in, *couldn't* let go, not until she was flexing around him in her release. He growled again as urgency filled him. The pleasure crept through him until it was all he could think about. He was close, so damned close. He bit down harder against her throat as his pace hit a crescendo, slamming into her so hard he could feel her entire body jerk in his hold.

Then she screamed, and he felt it, that moment he'd been waiting for. She clenched around him, milking him and promising him without words that it was okay to let go. He pulled back from her neck and shunted his hips forward one last time as a flood of heat and pleasure rushed through him, whiting out his vision. His body jerked again and again, conscious of nothing but how he felt until his vision gradually came back to him.

He panted into the night air as he came down from his high, his knot swelling inside her. It was a relief, the knot taking pressure off the parts of him that were now oversensitive from his release. He reached down, running his hands up and down her partially clad back. Her arms had collapsed against the ground, and he pulled her up against his chest, then fell back on his heels, allowing her to relax against him, to recover while his knot kept them locked together.

He nuzzled the spot where he'd bitten down, his chest warm with the realization that *this* was his mate. She was *here*.

And she's all mine.

Jess sat there in shock as the sweat cooled her skin, most of her focus on the weird pressure between her legs and the alien she'd just had sex with. They were still connected, his hands again roaming soothingly over her skin as he nuzzled against her neck, which was a little sore from him latching on.

In truth, a lot of her was sore. Her knees were hurting from grinding into the grass for so long, her throat was raw from the embarrassing noises she'd made, and her insides were sore from the pounding she'd taken and the ball of flesh that had inflated like a balloon after he'd come.

That's still *inflated,* she thought to herself as she started squirming in his hold, but it seemed he wasn't ready for the moment to end. He held her firmly on his lap, the pressure uncomfortably constant between her legs as they each came down from their individual highs. She could hear him panting behind her, his heavy breaths puffing against her ear, much as it had before all this had started. He wasn't saying anything, and for a moment, she even forgot that he could.

But that just gave her too much time to think, and there was one reality she just couldn't escape.

I don't know who he is.

He could be the enemy, though she highly doubted it at this point. The red skin and scales certainly leaned toward him being an ally, but she didn't *know.* And the only chance she *had* of knowing was asking him.

"Um," she said, but her voice came out as a hoarse wheeze, barely audible. She cleared her throat and tried again. "I hate to ask, but who are you?"

He tensed behind her, but then his soothing gestures increased in intensity. "I'm sorry. I should have introduced myself." He buried his face against her neck and hair, letting out a shaky breath. "It's just… this *thing…* I couldn't think."

Jess thought back to her first whiff of him, that growl that had turned her into heated butter, and she knew exactly what he meant. If he'd had a head start on that state of mind, she couldn't really blame him for not stopping to introduce himself. Hell, she hadn't exactly said, "I'm Jess," now had she?

She steeled up her courage and forced words into the awkward moment. "You know, don't worry about it. It's fine. Let's just… start fresh, okay?"

"Okay."

"I'm Jess, by the way."

"You can call me Davin. Commander Davin of the Drakonian military."

Drakonian. He's Drakoan.

She sighed in relief and relaxed against him. "Thank God."

"Oh?"

She chuckled. "Well, we *were* in the midst of an alien attack not that long ago…"

"You were worried I might be dangerous."

She tilted her head to the side to get a good look at him. He had a brow raised, and his mouth was tipped into the barest of grins. She smiled back, unable to help herself. "I'm sure you *are* dangerous, but at least you're not the enemy."

"True."

They fell silent for several more moments, and Jess was getting increasingly uncomfortable. Though she was growing to crave being in his arms, the bulb of flesh rearranging her insides was another story. "How long?"

"How long what?"

She pointed downward. "Until *that* goes down."

He looked up at the stars, seeming pensive. "It varies, but probably not long now. This isn't exactly the most conducive environment. It doesn't feel any smaller yet?"

"I don't know. Human men don't have that particular anatomic quirk, so I'm not used to feeling it. What is it?"

"A knot." He ran a finger along her cheek. "Is it uncomfortable?"

"Yes." She huffed. "Hell, yes."

"I'm sorry. Was it uncomfortable from the start or is it just lasting too long?"

She almost said it had *absolutely* been uncomfortable from the start, but then paused and admitted to herself that no, that would be a lie. In fact, at first, it had been fantastic. She shivered as she remembered how she'd come. Then before she'd even come down from her high, she'd felt him swelling. It had pressed up against something inside her, pushing her back up to her peak and holding her there for far too long. She didn't remember how long it had gone on for. She only remembered coming back to herself feeling completely boneless and exhausted, how he'd lifted her into his lap like a rag doll. It had taken long moments for her to even *feel* that knot again.

Maybe it's something I could get used to.

Because if she could get used to the after, it would be well worth it. That climax was the best she'd ever had. "No, it wasn't uncomfortable at first," she said finally, though her words seemed inadequate.

"Good."

"Davin?"

"Yes?"

"Why did we go mindless like that?"

He didn't respond at first, his movements suddenly tenser. "We're mates."

She racked her brain, but there were a lot of definitions of mates here on Earth, anything from friends to sexual partners to more. "And that means?"

He pulled her against his chest, holding her tight as she finally started to feel the swelling go down. "It's… biological. Drakoans know their mates by scent. It can make them… animalistic." He took in a deep, ragged breath, the air wafting over her exposed skin as he exhaled. "I… I'm sorry."

Trying to soothe him, she rubbed the arms that were holding her, a part of her loving the slightly abrasive texture of his scales. "It's not your fault."

"Nor is it yours. You didn't ask for this. I should have… had better control of myself."

She smirked, shaking her head. "I didn't exactly have a lot of control of myself either."

Jess leaned back, relaxing against his front, accepting the situation, at least for the time being.

But then movement caught her eye in the distance and she froze, suddenly very conscious of her partial nudity and the fact that she was still sitting on his dick.

"Davin?" she whispered, her focus on the vague form in the distance. It reminded her of the moment earlier that day when she'd first spotted Davin approaching their house. She remembered the curiosity and fear. This time, there was only fear, though. She was vulnerable, still trapped on Davin's lap while a mysterious someone approached in the darkness. She couldn't even so much as see the color of his skin or whether he had a tail. He was just an ominous shadow, and this time she didn't have a window between them. Hell, *this* time, she couldn't even run.

Her mind ran through possibilities at lightning speed, her

trepidation fueling her thoughts into greater and greater intensities.

Maybe it's a neighbor going for a walk.

Maybe it's one of Davin's team members coming to look for him.

Maybe they'll see me.

Maybe it's one of the bad aliens.

That last thought sent a chilling dread down her spine.

Please don't let it be a bad alien.

Please let it be friendly.

*D*avin felt Jess tense in his arms, and he immediately knew something was wrong.

"Davin?" she whispered, her voice quivering ever so slightly.

"Shhh," he said, but he was now on high alert, his gaze scouring his surroundings for threats. As he squinted into the night, his eyes adjusted, picking up heat signatures in the darkness. Most were small (animals) or horizontal (people sleeping). It only took him a moment to spot what had caught her attention.

A bipedal individual was walking in their direction. He tensed as well, his entire body wanting to react as his training had taught him, but he was at a disadvantage. He was currently locked to Jess, limiting his range of motion.

Davin reached for his pants, which were currently tangled around his legs. He fumbled and jerked at them until he managed to pull a weapon from its holster. He lifted and aimed, his other arm curling around Jess protectively, as if that would make any difference whatsoever.

"Are you really going to shoot me, Commander?" the approaching figure said.

Davin sagged as he let out a breath of relief, his gun arm falling to his side. "Damn it, Van. I could have shot you."

Van finally stepped out of the shadows, his stride sure as he crossed the street. "Would you have really shot me?"

Davin resisted the urge to growl at him. It wasn't Van's fault. *He'd* been the one to simply walk away. He was honestly surprised Van had come alone. It would have been perfectly within his rights to bring the entire team along to search for him. They were on a mission, after all. He *could* have thought something had happened to him. It could have been danger-ous. Van had taken one hell of a risk coming here on his own.

Then Davin was jarred from his thoughts as Jess finally squirmed away from him successfully, her pants pulled up her legs before he'd even missed her body heat.

Davin frowned as she stepped off to the side, curling her arms around her middle. He reached out, wanting to pull her into his embrace once more. But the moment he took a step to breach the distance between them, the mess of cloth and equipment around his legs tripped him up. He stopped to right his own clothing, but by the time he finished, Van laughed, drawing both their attentions.

It took several more long moments for Van to stop laughing, then to get his breathing under control. Even then, there was a slight wildness he wasn't used to seeing in his staid friend, Van shook his head, as if trying to shake off the episode, then looked to Jess before turning his assessing gaze back to Davin.

"So, this is her?"

Jess was trying desperately to tamp down on her embarrassment as the mystery man approached. Long moments later, he stepped into the light, and she could see that he was another Drakoan, like Davin. This alleviated at least *some* of her concerns, but she'd still been caught, literally, with her pants down. That had never happened to her before. Hell, she'd never even participated in the time-honored tradition of the "Walk of Shame."

Which was probably why it took her brain so long to register that Davin had called him by *name*. He *knew* him. Who was he? Was he a friend? A rival? A subordinate? Davin *had* said he was a commander, right? That sounded like a pretty high up position.

As her mind was scrambling through *that* endless series of questions, she noticed that the pressure that had kept her distracted and uncomfortable for so long was finally gone. Unwilling to wait a second longer, she awkwardly scrambled to her feet and jerked on her yoga pants.

Then the newcomer, Van, said something about her, and she snapped her head up.

What's going on?

She turned to Davin, hoping for answers, but he was quiet as he, too, donned his pants. The awkwardness of the moment was amplified as they each failed to fill the silence. Jess's gaze jumped from Davin to Van and back again, expecting *someone* to say *something*. But Davin's friend seemed content to simply stare at him, as if that alone could mine the answers he sought.

What answers was he looking for?

Had Davin done something wrong?

They stared each other down like two gunslingers, causing the already uncomfortable moment to drag on longer and longer.

At first, Jess had her arms wrapped around her middle, feeling embarrassed by being caught in such a compromising and vulnerable position. But as the moment stretched into infinity, her death grip on her ribs gradually loosened. She stared the two down, trying to piece together this unspoken puzzle she found herself in the middle of, but it was useless. Davin seemed mostly defensive, probably at being caught like that, and his friend was as easy to read as a brick wall, giving nothing away.

Finally, she got fed up. "Okay, what the fuck is going on? Who are you?" She pointed at the new guy, firing off questions as fast as her lips could move. "Why are you here? Why are you angry with him?"

He turned to her, his gaze inscrutable, then turned back to Davin as if all answers lay with him.

She turned to him as well, a sinking feeling of dread settling into her gut. The entire scene felt so ominous. The dark and quiet street, the shadows, the mystery figure, being outnumbered. A part of her just wanted to go inside and forget all this ever happened. Hell, what she *really* wanted was for the world to make sense again, but that was never going to happen. The world had changed and nothing said she had to like it.

Jess frowned, curling her arms around her torso once again. She was starting to feel a slight chill, and she wasn't sure if it was the weather or the situation.

"She's my mate," Davin finally said, breaching the silence.

A frown slowly stretched across Van's face, somehow managing to darken the red scales there. "I guessed as much."

Davin paused, a weird expression crossing his face, then continued with the introductions. "Van, this is Jess. Jess, this is Van, my second in command."

"Delighted," she said, the uncomfortable situation making her snarky.

"I'm guessing Van came looking for me after I came here."

Van stiffened, a volatile expression briefly crossing his face before he got it under control once more. "Once you *disappeared*, you mean. I finished that report for you, then when I came back outside, you were gone. No word, no nothing. You don't do that on mission. What the hell were you thinking?"

"I wasn't."

Van scoffed. "Clearly."

"Don't start," Davin snapped, taking a step forward. "You have no idea what this is like."

"You're right. I don't. Because you haven't said a damned word." Van was now animated, throwing his hands about as he threw accusations at Davin. Something about the display felt wrong, though. She didn't know the man, but there'd been something a hell of a lot more stalwart in his posture when he'd first approached. Now the restraints were gone, and he held nothing back. "I'm your second in command, damnit. I need to know these things. Hell, I'm your friend. I *deserve* to know these things."

"What could I do?" Davin said in return, meeting him shout for shout. They'd been slowly creeping closer and closer. Now, they were practically toe to toe.

Jess almost wished she had some popcorn now that the discomfort of earlier was gone and the dam had broken between the two friends.

"You could have told me!"

"And do what?"

"I don't know!"

"Exactly!"

They seemed to run out of things to say, but that didn't stop them from staring each other down like two guard dogs, both at the ends of their chains.

Entertainment over, she knew she needed to stop this. An argument could be productive, but this certainly wasn't.

But what could she do? She was half afraid they would lash out at her if she tried to intervene. Again, the fighting dogs analogy came to mind.

What would she do if it were two human men fighting? She threw out idea after idea before one stuck.

Well, it's better than nothing.

She opened her mouth and gave it a try. "Okay, I feel like I'm missing something. Are you two lovers or something?"

They both balked, jerking away from each other as if they'd been burned, causing her to smile triumphantly.

Well, some things are universal.

Van straightened, facing her as he adjusted his uniform, smoothing down lines that were already pretty much straight. His demeanor returned to that more composed mode he'd been in when he'd first walked into the light only a few minutes before. Davin took a steadying breath, but couldn't seem to look at her.

Jess stepped forward, compassion making her want to pull the two men into her arms for a hug. "Why don't we start from the beginning? Okay?"

"All right. What do you know?" Van said hesitantly.

"Personally or globally?" she said with a chuckle, trying to further break the tension.

"Globally, I guess."

She searched for a smile, but Van was a tough cookie to crack, so she shrugged it off and started talking. "Okay. A couple weeks ago, the President went on TV announcing that a hostile alien fleet had reached Earth. He declared a State of Emergency and asked all nonessential workers to stay in their homes when at all possible. There were the usual assurances. 'Everything is handled, everyone's cooperating, there's no reason to fear.'" She shook her head and leaned forward. "Let me tell you, it didn't work."

Jess frowned, trying to remember exactly how things had gone after that. She'd mostly heard things in rumors and often out of order, the events happening too fast to keep up with. Not that she'd ever been one to keep up with current events. Generally, if it didn't happen in the gaming world, she wasn't interested, but some of her roommates were. "Let's see, after that, there was the requisite panic-buying, stories about nationwide shortages on certain things. Some of my room-mates were constantly checking for updates, but it felt like it was a lot of the same, over and over again, so I wasn't exactly paying much attention myself." She shrugged. "Then the power went out. That was days ago."

"Was there any rioting? Looting?"

"I don't know. Why?"

"On our trek to the US Capitol and White House, we spotted damage that didn't seem consistent with an organized attack."

"Well, I wouldn't be surprised, but we're a few miles out, so I'm not sure we would have heard if it happened after the power outage."

He nodded.

"So, what do *you* know?"

"About the same time your received the announcement from your government, we received orders to deploy to Earth to reinforce an ally, humans, who were currently under threat of attack. We arrived a few days ago just in time to witness the use of a weapon unlike any we'd ever seen before. It knocked out all our sensors temporarily. When we got them back online, the enemy forces we'd detected upon first arriving were gone. We were able to initiate communication with the remaining human ships in orbit, but neither we nor they could reach anyone on Earth." He sighed. "Apparently, those massive weapons not only took out the entire enemy fleet, they also took out Earth's satellite communications network."

"Nuclear bombs," Jess said in shock.

"Yes, I believe that's what they said it was."

A part of her couldn't believe it. No one had used a nuclear bomb in an offensive capacity since World War II. It was the ultimate deterrent, but no one *actually* wanted to use them. They were too nasty, had too much collateral damage. And yet it made sense. Nuclear bombs created EMPs. If it detonated low enough to affect Earth, even a single bomb could wreck havoc on a massive territory. "An HEMP," she muttered to herself.

"What?"

"An HEMP. High-altitude electromagnetic pulse."

"Of course," Van said, looking a little excited. "That makes perfect sense." He started pacing. "We couldn't understand why the power hadn't been brought back online, why communications systems were still offline. We assumed the damage to the satellite network was to blame, but if the electronics *themselves* were fried, going back online again would be no simple task."

"But I would have thought the government would be prepared for that. I mean, we've known about EMPs since like the 1950s. Wouldn't all their equipment be shielded or something?"

Van stopped pacing. "That's true. Even if the main power grid was damaged, they should have been able to maintain command *somewhere*. But where?"

"Fuck if I know."

Van turned and nodded to her. "Thank you. You have been most helpful."

A little thrill ran through her at being called helpful, but she shrugged, trying to pass it off as no big deal.

He turned to Davin, who'd been quiet this entire time. "Come. We have to go."

Davin tensed, and Jess knew what he was going to say next. "I'm not going anywhere." He looked to Jess, his expression one part stubborn, one part pleading.

"Davin, my friend, you have to come back. I can only cover for you for so long. You are the Commander of the Drakonian fleet here. Everyone is looking to you for direction."

Jess startled at his words.

Oh my God, I forgot.

A cold sensation rushed through her, leaving a twinge of guilt in its wake. He'd *said* he was a commander, but she hadn't really thought that concept through to its inevitable conclusion. She'd realized he was important, but not that people would *need* him. *She'd* been reassured by knowing he was somebody, someone of power, of influence, of control. At the time, it had been nothing but a word, something to anchor him to the real world in her mind, but it was more than that, wasn't it? It was his duty and a heavy weight upon his shoulders than no one else could carry but him. People *relied* on him.

And so long as he's here, he's letting them down.

"No, I can't," Davin insisted, his voice getting deliciously growly as he inched closer to her.

"Davin, please. You must."

But with each pleading word from his friend, Davin became more adamant, more intractable. Van tried reason, duty, emotion. Nothing worked, and each entreaty had Davin inching closer and closer to her. When he was practically on top of her, it finally clicked.

The mating.

That was why he was here, after all, in her yard. But that wasn't why he was on Earth. Both he and Van were in uniform, both with weapons clipped into holsters. Even in the dark, it was easy enough to clock them as soldiers, soldiers on a mission. And so long as they stayed in her front yard arguing, they wouldn't be fulfilling that mission, a mission she suspected was essential to getting Earth back on her feet again.

I need to do something.

But what? What could *she* do? She was just a content creator online. And even *that* was beyond her abilities right now because there was no internet, no computers, no electricity. She was literally *useless* right now.

And yet she was worse than that, wasn't she? She was actually less than nothing. She was a negative because she was holding up this team of aliens from doing their jobs. Without her, Davin would be doing what he was supposed to be doing. He would be leading his team, helping Earth get back on her feet.

But how do I fix this?

That was the question, wasn't it? So long as she was here, Davin wouldn't leave her side.

So I go with him.

The idea struck like a lightning bolt, both painfully obvious and terrifying. She didn't know what their mission was or if it was dangerous. And while she'd reassured Scottie that she could take care of herself, she felt far less confident in this situation. She was no soldier, and her martial arts training was rusty at best. Would she even react correctly in a real fight?

She frowned and cringed as she blurted out, "Let me go with you," as if she were ripping off a bandage.

"What?" they said in unison, jerking around to face her.

"Let me go with you," she said, this time with more confidence.

But they were each looking at her like she was crazy.

Shit.

This isn't working.

Think, Jess, think.

What would convince them?

"I know the area? I might be able to help?"

Van stared at her for several moments, his gaze calculating. Then his eyes widened slightly, a grin twitching at the corners of his lips. He gave Jess a barely discernible nod before diverting his attention to Davin. The moment they both saw Davin calm, she knew she'd won him over too.

Van nodded. "Let's go."

EPISODE THIRTEEN

For Her Safety

*V*an latched onto Davin's arm the moment they started walking, holding him back so they could talk, a talk Davin had been avoiding all day.

To make matters worse, he could physically *feel* every foot of distance separating them as Jess got farther and farther ahead. It felt wrong, and he wanted to close the distance, but Van wouldn't be budged.

"Do you have any idea how bad your timing is?" Van said, his voice barely raising above a whisper.

Davin laughed. Yes, he knew, but there were just some things in life you couldn't control and this was one of them. He wished he could have just pretended it didn't happen, that he hadn't caught her scent, but Drakoans weren't built that way. They'd developed entire classes of medications exactly *because* there was essentially no controlling themselves once that instinct kicked in. So when it had happened to him, he'd tried. He'd honestly tried, but he'd barely been able to think, and the moment he'd let down his guard, he'd succumbed. "I'm sorry."

Van sighed, a compassionate expression crossing his face as his voice softened. "You could have told me. I'm your friend, Davin."

"I know," he said as a lot of the tension drained from his body. They'd been friends for years. They'd risen up the ranks together. If he'd been thinking, he *would* have told him.

But then he frowned. His memories were a bit murky, but he could swear he remembered specifically saying "mate" early on. It had been under his breath, but hadn't Van asked him about it? His brain gnawed at the memory like an old bone, but with most of the day a hazy mess in his recollection, he wasn't entirely sure.

Van sighed, drawing Davin's attention and keeping him away from another thought spiral. "You can't take her with you everywhere. You realize that, right?"

A part of him instinctually reeled back, but it didn't have the same sway over him that it had earlier in the day. Slowly, he responded. "Yeah. Of course."

Van shook his head, looking a little bewildered. "And yet you wouldn't leave her behind. She's safe at home, Davin. She's safer there than anywhere else."

Davin flinched, then his ire rose like a tsunami, and he snapped. "She's safe with *me*!"

"No, she's not," Van barked back, getting in Davin's face before seemingly remembering himself and pulling back to recover his calm. He took a deep breath, then continued. "We have no idea what's going to happen. We have no idea what's out there. But if there is a threat, it'll probably encounter us first, and as long as she's with us, she'll be in danger if that happens."

"It's... not that simple."

Jess was far enough ahead now that he could think more clearly, her scent not clouding his mind. He knew rationally that Van was right, but he still couldn't bring himself to be separated from her. A desperate part of him kept insisting that she was only safe with *him,* even though he knew intellectually that it wasn't true. He could feel the pull of it, the urgency, the agonizing need that wouldn't let go. "I just… can't."

"You *can,*" Van insisted, turning to face him. "You must. Davin, it's for her own good. Hell, it's for the good of the entire planet. The faster we finish our mission, the faster her life can return to normal."

"And the faster we go home." That thought was like a kick in the chest, knocking the air from his lungs.

The faster we finish our mission, the less time I have to convince her.

He was supposed to go *home,* to *Koa,* when all this was done. Would Jess want to come with him? He wasn't sure. He needed time, but his conscience ate at him for even thinking that. Giving himself time meant leaving countless humans in desperate situations. He couldn't do that, could he? He couldn't be that selfish, could he?

That's not me.

It can't be.

I'm a good man.

I'm a good soldier.

"Exactly. The only reason we're here is to support Earth. Once she's on her feet again, our jobs are done." Van sighed. "I know that doesn't sound the most appealing to you right now, but it's our reality, Davin. We don't have a choice."

Davin shook his head, still not quite ready to give up even though he knew it was wrong. "I just need time." The protest was weak, even to his own ears.

"Would it make any difference?" Van said, his voice gentle.

"What?" He looked up at Van, who was giving him a compassionate expression that made his heart lurch in his chest with emotion. That was *not* the expression of a supportive friend. That was an expression of condolence, of empathy and grief. "Don't," he snapped out in desperation.

"Davin…"

He shrugged Van's hand off and started stomping away, disgusted with even the *look* of his friend right now. "No."

"Davin!" Van barked. A moment later, his hand latched onto Davin's arm, this time yanking him backward. Once Davin was facing him once more, this time completely stopped, his voice dropped to barely a whisper, while Davin fumed back at him. "You can't control her actions. You can't make her want you. You know how this usually goes on Koa. She doesn't even have the benefit of our background, our knowledge. She can't possibly know what's going on."

"She does," he said through gritted teeth. "I told her."

"And she understood? Do you think she *really* understands? Do you think it's even *possible* that she could understand?"

A chill ran through him at Van's words. They were the things he'd been trying not to think about. He'd been trying not to think about how often biological matings were rejected on Koa, telling himself that was cultural, that it wouldn't happen here. He'd tried to tell himself that she would understand. And he'd absolutely refused to think of the *future*.

But Van wasn't letting him live in that little bubble anymore, that fantasy world of his own making. He was *determined* to bring Davin back to the real world, a world where people were without power, possibly without food and running water. A real world where anarchy was only a breath away. His mission was *vital* to ensuring that Earth returned to normal, that life here was returned to its former glory. He didn't want to hear that, though. He didn't want to think about it because it made the things he was feeling right now a hindrance and morally bankrupt.

What's worse, his feelings, this mating, were actively *hurting* his mate. This was her home. If he focused on her, her home would continue to be without power. She would have to live in a world under constant danger of falling into chaos. How long would she survive like that? Months? Weeks?

"Davin?"

"I shouldn't have let her come with us."

"Yes. I know." Van nodded. "She only came because you refused."

"What?"

"She only came because you refused. Although, I'll admit, I didn't figure it out the very *moment* she offered, but it became pretty clear she was trying to get you to do the right thing."

Davin sagged, the statement gutting him. "So she didn't even want to come with us. She's potentially risking her safety because I'm a useless ass?"

"I wouldn't go that far, but yeah."

He shook his head as pain bloomed, nearly suffocating him. "I have to let her go."

"Yeah."

Every part of his body felt locked in place, like it was unwilling to admit the truth. It took great effort to slowly relax each muscle. He unclenched his hands, his arms, legs, torso, and finally his jaw. "I don't want to," he said, a final plaintive cry before defeat inevitably dug its sharp claws into him for good.

Van shifted his hand, gripping Davin's shoulder comfortingly. "I know, but it's the right thing to do."

Jess tried to ignore the fact that Davin and Van were behind her, talking quietly together like two teenage girls sharing gossip. It was a bit awkward, and she really wanted to be closer to Davin, but she suspected the two needed time to talk. She'd only just met him, but she was certain something wasn't quite right with him. You didn't get to be someone as high up as a commander without a certain degree of professionalism and discipline, discipline he seemed completely lacking in since meeting her.

Because of our mating.

She couldn't say she completely understood the mating. She could *feel* it, but it seemed simultaneously awe inspiring and baffling. How could two species that had no evolutionary common origin click so well together? How could a biological quirk of one species affect another completely unrelated one? It was so weird, but also fascinating.

And why was it that she could literally *feel* every foot of distance between them, like a string tugging on her belly button? She reached down, touching the spot in question. Though, she supposed the sensation wasn't that distinct or specific. It was more like a nagging thought in the back of her mind, foggy but annoyingly persistent.

She glanced back. The others were now over a block behind her, and she stopped. Van had his hand on Davin's arm, and they were talking intensely. Then his hand moved to Davin's shoulder and all the energy oozed out of the conversation.

Something just happened.

She wanted to smile in relief at the tension finally breaking, but she didn't quite feel relief in that moment. Instead, her gut churned with anxiety like whatever had just been decided wasn't good for *her*. She didn't know why she felt that way, but she did, so she turned around and started moving toward the shuttle once more. It wasn't that far now. In fact, she could see the first glimpses of the trees in the distance. It would probably be just another couple blocks.

Jess picked up her pace, eager to get this over with and put some distance between her and whatever decision those two had made. She focused, instead, on her surroundings. They were in a quiet neighborhood filled with boxy brick homes. Most had cars parked in the driveways, possibly never to be used again because the government had been dumb enough to launch nuclear bombs in their moment of desperation.

What had they been thinking? The whole point of nuclear bombs was *not* to use them. They were a threat, the ultimate threat, but she couldn't imagine anyone other than a psycho actually considering putting them in play.

And how many *did* they use? How much of the world had been affected? Had it been an accident? Had just a single bomb detonated too low, causing this mess? But then, why wouldn't someone have come to the rescue by now? If it had only been one bomb, wouldn't other countries or FEMA or something come in to provide support?

Wait, Van had said they couldn't reach *anyone* on Earth. He'd mentioned the satellite grid being knocked out, but that shouldn't have knocked out *all* communication, right? There should have been back-up systems, maybe radios or something. Those satellites hadn't existed back when the space program had first started. Whatever they'd used, it would have been slower, most likely, but they definitely could have tested that out in the time between the power going out and them coming down to Earth to investigate. Did that mean *everyone* was affected by the EMP?

Holy shit.

Jess slowed as a chill ran through her, her stomach churning anew.

How the fuck are we gonna come back from this?

She looked around, at the quiet street that got more eerie the longer she thought about *why* it was so quiet. Ordinarily, it wouldn't be this quiet. There wouldn't be so many cars in the driveways. There would be people out socializing, going to bars or game nights. There would be people working night shifts. There would be lights on, people watching late night shows or streaming their favorite movies. People would be online playing video games. It would *not* be this dark, this quiet. There should be lights pouring out of windows. She should be able to hear music or conversations drifting on the warm summer air.

Instead, there was nothing. It was almost as if the world had ended, and she was the only one left. That chill from before ran down her spine, and she picked up her pace, jogging as she finally stepped onto the grassy park lawn. Pretty quickly, she spotted the shuttle. It stood out like a sore thumb in the sea of green, and she beelined for it.

It took only moments before she was slowing directly in front of it. She stopped and turned around, spotting her companions in the distance, even farther away than before. She had to wait for them to catch up.

When they finally arrived, Davin wouldn't look at her, so she turned to Van.

"So?"

"We were talking."

She smirked. "I could tell."

"We think you should go home."

She paused. Her knee jerk reaction was to protest. She'd just arrived, after all. It seemed ridiculous to just turn back around and go home, but then she turned to Davin. There was a bit of a defeated air to him, but seeing him now also made her remember why she'd come in the first place.

To make him do the right thing.

"You're okay with this?" She watched him closely, looking for any signs that he would act up again, but this barely looked like the same man. There was no outrage this time, but he also didn't look happy either. Honestly, he looked miserable. She was tempted to comfort him, to pull him into her arms and rock him back and forth until he was in a better mood, but she was afraid that might set back their progress.

"Yes," he finally said. He looked at her for a brief moment, but that moment was enough. She could *see* the struggle in his eyes. This was not an easy decision for him, and she resisted the urge to smile.

Jess kept her face composed, but inside, she was practically jumping up and down, and she blamed it on the mating. She didn't *want* this to be an easy decision for him. She *wanted* him to struggle because this was a struggle for her as well, and she didn't want this to be over so soon. Though she had no way of knowing where this would go, she did want it to go *somewhere*, and she hoped, when all this was said and done, that he would come back to her.

"And you're just going to continue with your mission? You're not going to come after me?" She had mixed feelings as she spoke those words into existence. She *wanted* him to come after her, but she *knew* he needed to stay away. Earth needed him, after all, and she just wasn't selfish enough to ignore that.

"No." He shook his head jerkily. "The mission comes first."

Jess nodded slowly, surprised by the slice of hurt that flared up when he said those words, but she shoved it down ruthlessly. She'd already decided on this path. She had no right to be upset. The mission *was* more important, she reminded herself. If he were an American soldier, she would want him to put the mission first when he was on active duty, wouldn't she? She wouldn't want his head to be filled with her, putting him, his team, and his mission at risk, would she? "Okay," she said finally. "Well, good luck. I hope to see you again soon. Stay safe, Davin."

They both paused for a moment, neither of them willing to turn away.

I should walk away.

It's time to walk away.

"Should I walk you home?" he asked, looking off into the night, then back at her.

An awkward laugh snapped out of her, and she shook her head. "No, I think that would be a bad idea."

No, they needed a clean break, and this seemed the best time for it.

Davin nodded, accepting her decision and taking a step back, as if he needed that physical reminder not to follow.

Jess turned, putting her back to him. Those first steps were hard. She could feel that imaginary string stretching with each step, and as she started walking, she could also feel their eyes on her. It was a feeling that never quite went away, not even when she unlocked her front door and went inside. It was both comforting and creepy.

Was it just her imagination, though? Was walking through the empty night just playing tricks on her mind?

Or was it wishful thinking? A part of her kind of liked the idea of Davin being there to protect her if some ne'er-do-well jumped out of the shadows, but he'd told her he wouldn't. He'd essentially promised. Would he break a promise like that?

She honestly couldn't believe he would. Though she barely knew him, she'd already formed a picture of him in her mind that was both honorable and kind. She couldn't imagine someone like that going back on their word or stalking behind someone in the night without their knowledge.

And yet, that idea plagued her as she walked quietly upstairs and settled into bed. She couldn't quite escape it as she stared at the ceiling, willing herself to sleep. The popcorn texture formed patterns over her head as thoughts swirled in her brain, tormenting her with possibilities, both good and bad. By the time she finally succumbed to exhaustion, one thought was floating on repeat through her mind.

Do I even want *him to keep his promise?*

EPISODE FOURTEEN

Just a Little Light Stalking

*Y*ou're doing the right thing.

Those were the words Van had spoken as they'd both watched Jess walk away. They continued to ring through his head even now, hours later, as he lay in his bunk, trying to fall asleep.

But sleep was an evasive bitch, and all he found himself doing was tossing and turning, tangling himself in his blankets until he had to straighten them once again.

Davin huffed, then sat up and calmly rearranged the fabric until his own bodyweight wasn't tying his legs to the bed. He couldn't quite bring himself to lie down again, though. This was the sixth time in only a couple hours. There were many more hours to go before the sun greeted him once more.

He looked over to the other side of the room, where his friend was out cold. Van wasn't so much as moving a muscle, and Davin envied him that. He yearned for the bliss of oblivion, but that wasn't to be. He sighed, giving up on sleep, and carefully threw back the covers, not wanting to make a noise with Van only a couple feet away. There was no reason they both had to suffer from insomnia tonight.

The bed creaked ominously as he shifted his weight. He hesitated, waiting to see if his roommate would wake, but Van didn't so much as twitch, so he continued. His bare feet made nary a noise in the quiet of night. And after a few brief moments, he'd collected his things and stopped in front of the door. Worried the door might wake Van, he looked back. He knew the door would make a noise when it opened. There was nothing he could do about that. He kept his eye on Van as he lifted his hand, activated it, and flinched as the control panel beeped, then the door whooshed open.

Davin held his breath. Several moments ticked by, but Van only took a deep, even breath, then settled in once more. Davin crept backward, relief washing through him as the door closed without incident, leaving him in the dimly lit hallway. He looked both ways, but wasn't sure where to go. He hadn't thought this through that much. All he'd been thinking about was the hours of restlessness that lay before him and feeling so uncomfortable, it was almost painful.

He could go to the bridge, maybe check the mission documents, come up with a strategy, but after considering it for only a moment, he dismissed it. He was still suffering the lingering effects of his time with Jess. What could he possibly get done when his brain just refused to focus?

Unfortunately, that didn't leave him a lot of options. The only places he could go were the bridge, the med bay, and outside. If he stayed inside, there was also the risk that he would wake someone. Sound tended to carry in vessels like this. Too much metal, too close confines. Hell, even on a big ship, the sound carried because everything was made of metal. The only places protected from it were the patient rooms, which were soundproofed to ensure adequate rest for healing. In fact, sometimes personnel would check themselves into the med bay just for insomnia. It was the only quiet place in the entire ship.

He shook his head. "I really can't think straight right now, can I? Here I've been worrying about making too much noise, but we're all used to sleeping in noisy places, aren't we? This is nothing."

It was actually kind of funny, really. He shook his head, then headed toward the bridge, a slight smile on his face. And even though it likely didn't matter, he carefully set his boots on the floor before sitting down.

Just in case.

The echoing silence and unnatural stillness of the night kept him sitting there doing nothing for quite a while, and it even managed to distract him from the problem at hand.

But soon enough, he was shaking his head and pulling up the display panel attached to the armrest to try to get some work done. He tapped away at the screen, trying to focus on reading messages, responding to them, giving orders, etc., but he kept having to read the same sentences over and over again. And when he went to type, he would find himself staring at the screen, his mind blank and unable to form words.

Finally giving up, he pushed the display away and stared out the window, out at the stretch of greenery they'd parked in. In the dark, it seemed both striking and dangerous. There was an uneasiness about the view, like the shadows were shifting and creeping, threatening to consume everything in their path.

And I sent Jess out into that.

He shook his head. "Stop it," he whispered to himself sternly. "She's fine. Don't do this to yourself." But as he lifted his gaze back to the view outside, he couldn't help thinking about Jess, his mate. Her ample curves. Her lean muscles. Her tan skin. Her long, soft hair.

The way she feels underneath me.

"Stop it." He took in a shaky breath. Where before, the distance had given him a little bit of clarity to think, now it seemed to be working against him. Without her in sight, he had only his memories, what few there were. The air felt wrong without her scent in it. And without the distraction the others served, he could feel the full pull of her, like someone was trying to rip pieces off of him.

What if she never made it home?

What if she's not safe?

This time, he couldn't quite bring himself to say stop it because he didn't know. Anything could have happened to her since she left his side. How would he know? He had no way of checking.

You can *check.*

He paused. Van would be pissed at him, for sure, but no one had to know, right? He could just make the quick walk to her place, make sure she was okay, then return. Quick and easy. Van and the team would be sound asleep in their beds. They would never miss him. He could be back at the shuttle long before anyone woke up. Easy.

"Yeah," he said under his breath as he nodded to himself. "Easy."

Davin stood up, collecting his boots from the floor, then silently left the bridge and walked down the hallway to the back door. He looked behind him one last time before opening it, just to make sure no one was awake.

Just a quick check. Then I'll be right back.

No one needs to know.

When Davin arrived, he was relieved that her scent trail ran straight up to her front door, meaning she'd likely made it home safely. He then wandered around the building, but none of the downstairs bedrooms were hers, leaving his only options to assume she was safe or start climbing.

"You did what you said you'd do, Davin," he told to himself, but he couldn't quite bring himself to leave. Instead, he found himself standing in the road in front of her home, staring up at the edifice as his night vision distorted his view. Everything looked oddly stark, with little flares of heat highlighted against the duller backdrop. He counted six bodies in the house.

Who were they?

Was she safe with them?

Then a chill wind swept over him, and he shivered, his protective instincts flaring up. He took a step forward unconsciously, but then stopped himself.

No, I can't go in there.

He clenched his fists, his entire body tense as the urge to go in and keep her warm held him in its sway. He *needed* to make sure she was okay, but he knew he couldn't. She wouldn't appreciate that. But he couldn't help wondering. Was she warm enough? Did she have enough blankets? Was she shivering? As he scoured the building, he could see no heat sources other than sleeping people.

She only has her own body heat to keep her warm.

That's not right.

She deserves better.

His heart constricted as emotion struck him, freezing him in place. He should leave, go back to the shuttle, wait for his team to wake up. He shouldn't stand around outside her house making a nuisance of himself. It wasn't right, and he knew it, but he couldn't seem to get himself to budge. He could keep himself from moving forward, but he just couldn't force himself to walk away.

The longer he stood there, the more the cold night seeped into him and the more his most intrusive thoughts got the better of him. From the road, he eventually identified each of the six scent profiles in the house. Four females, two males.

Scenting the males almost had his instincts overriding his sense, especially since one of the scents was familiar. It was part of Jess's scent, meaning the male was close to her, close enough to rub his scent off on her. But who was he? Why had he touched *Davin's* mate? Even though the two were clearly in separate beds and were probably nothing more than house-mates, he imagined the two being intimate, touching, hugging, kissing, cuddling.

His anger spiked with each intrusive scenario that popped into his head, even while he tried desperately to counter them with logic. But logic couldn't stop the thoughts from popping into his brain. Each thought further cemented him to the spot, preventing him from leaving.

Before long, the heat signatures started to dim. Alarmed, he took a step forward, unable to stop himself as increasingly warm light gave extra dimensions to the place his mate called home. He could see the little bits of damage, the peeling paint, a tree branch that had fallen on the roof.

And now, without being able to see Jess's heat signature, he couldn't quite stop himself from taking a few more steps forward, his feet taking him up and underneath her window on autopilot. His neck craned up as light and shadow played against the siding.

Warmth touched his skin, but he barely noticed, just as he'd barely noticed the chill that had seeped into his bones.

All that mattered was making sure she was okay.

All that mattered was *Jess*.

EPISODE FIFTEEN

Invasion of Privacy

*J*ess woke feeling refreshed, but as if something was missing. She had the impulse to reach behind her, as if she expected someone to be there, but why would she expect that? She hadn't slept next to anyone in ages.

An image of Davin popped into her head, and she jerked upright, her blankets dropping around her waist. The room was full of morning light, and she could hear her friends moving around in other portions of the house. That should have all been perfectly normal and familiar, but nothing felt familiar today. Everything felt different, almost *wrong*. She thought of Davin, and she wished she'd been able to stay with him, but she understood why he'd suggested she leave. He needed to focus. He had a job to do. *She* didn't.

Yet still, the yearning was there. The *need* was there. She glanced out her window, but being on the second floor, all she could see were branches and one corner of the neighbor's house.

He's not there, she told herself, but she couldn't quite ignore her instincts. They were lying to her, of course. She knew that, but she couldn't help feeling that if she just got up and looked down, Davin would be there.

Don't be stupid.

He's back at the shuttle.

He can't be outside.

He promised.

No, that was just wishful thinking, and as she got out of bed, she forced herself not to look out and down at the space below her window. Instead, she went through the motions, halfheartedly throwing on clothes and tossing her hair back into a ponytail without looking. She barely took in her surroundings as she stepped out into the hall and trudged downstairs. She was tensing slightly as she made her way deeper into the shared spaces of the house, even less motivated to interact with someone than she'd been to get dressed.

Unfortunately, in a house with five other people, avoiding them was essentially impossible. There was always someone underfoot.

"Morning, Jess," Inez said quietly as they crossed paths at the base of the stairs.

Jess sighed.

Thank God for small favors.

Of all the people to bump into this morning, Inez was probably the best. She was quiet and good at reading a person's mood. You could always rely on her to give you what you needed, whether it was a thoughtful comment, a compassionate ear, or plenty of space.

Jess nodded and moved on, yearning for a quiet spot to sit and think.

Then maybe you should have just stayed in your room.

She frowned as she slipped into the empty living room. Sure, she *could* have stayed in her bedroom, but then the impulse to think of Davin or look out the window would have plagued her constantly. Even now, the impulse remained, but it was a little easier to control here.

And yet, there were reminders here, too. This was the room where she'd seen him yesterday. She looked out the window, imagining his form in the late afternoon rays. The lighting was all wrong, which helped, but his memory was like a ghost in her mind, never quite there but never quite leaving either.

"What am I gonna do?" she whispered to herself. It didn't seem healthy the way she couldn't seem to stop thinking about him, but he'd talked about mates, about how it was instinctual, biological. Clearly, that was happening here, because she really didn't know him from Adam.

And she knew full well that biology could be a powerful beast. She'd known plenty of people with other neurotypes, had seen how it affected them.

But her own brain had always been consistently dependable. She'd never needed to pay much attention to it. She'd never before had to suffer through the experience of not being fully in control of her own mind and body.

It was unnerving, and she didn't like it.

But it didn't matter what she liked or didn't like. She couldn't change how she felt, or how her mind and body seemed to be working right now. Even when she closed her eyes and tried to clear her mind, a practice she'd been doing all her life, thoughts of Davin popped up unbidden again and again. And it wasn't like the normal thoughts she was used to. Usually, she could imagine a river in her mind and just watch as the thoughts rolled on down the river and out of sight. But thoughts of Davin were like a siege. They ignored the river, rushing forward and demanding to be seen, to be heard. They ignored all attempts to "walk away" or move on.

"This is definitely not healthy," she muttered under her breath.

Then a commotion broke out in another portion of the house. She jerked her eyes open, her entire body tensing in anticipation. "Guys?" she said as she leaned forward in her seat. "What's going on?"

Then Amanda rushed in through the doorway. Alarmed, Jess jumped to her feet and ran to her side. "Amanda, what's wrong?"

Her face was ashen, her eyes wide. Her mouth opened and closed like a fish out of water for a few moments before she spoke. "Inez saw an alien lurking in the yard."

Dread washed through her, and it felt like the moment they'd all been fearing had finally arrived. But Jess refused to let fear get the better of her.

Maybe it's not an alien.

Maybe Inez didn't get a good look.

"Where?" Jess said, urgency calling her to action.

"Outside her room," she stuttered, her hands fluttering up and over her mouth.

Jess nodded, awkwardly wondering if she should offer comfort, but then decided investigating was the more practical choice. "Come on." She urged Amanda forward. "Let's go figure this out." Hopefully, someone else could look after Amanda while she got to the bottom of this. "It's probably nothing," she said in a halfhearted gesture of comfort.

But it didn't feel like nothing. Her adrenaline was surging, and Amanda's trudging pace was setting her teeth on edge. She wanted to rush to the back of the house and demand someone explain what they'd seen, but she couldn't do that with Amanda holding her back.

So instead, possibilities flooded her mind. At first, she thought it could be Davin or someone on his team, but she easily dismissed that. He'd promised he wouldn't, and she couldn't imagine Van showing up unless Davin had broken his promise. She didn't know the rest of his team, but she had to believe they were just as reliable as Van. None of them had any reason to lurk outside Inez's window.

Unfortunately, the other options she was coming up with weren't anywhere near as appealing. Enemy aliens. Creeps. Peeping Toms. Looters. Thieves. As she made her way to Inez's room, she got to where she was almost *hoping* it was Davin and his team, because nothing else she came up with had anywhere near as good of an outcome.

When they finally reached the room, Melissa was cradling Inez and trying (and failing) to calm her down while glaring at Thom and Scottie, who were currently arguing. *They* were the ones creating the commotion. They were in each other's faces, leaning in and looking ready to come to blows.

"Hey, knock it off!" Jess snapped, forgetting about Amanda for a moment as she rushed across the room and pushed the two men apart. "What the fuck, dudes?"

Thom crossed his arms, cooly glaring at Scottie while Scottie pouted and looked to Jess for validation.

"Oh, don't even start. I have no idea what you two were fighting about."

"Thom is being unreasonable."

She frowned at Scottie, suspecting the reverse was probably true. Thom was reasonable to a fault. She couldn't imagine him being the unreasonable one. Scottie, on the other hand, occasionally got riled up and forgot to listen. It was usually endearing, but sometimes it caused trouble. "Thom?"

"I suggested we stay inside, away from the windows. It is unlikely that anyone outside would be targeting us specifically, so the smartest choice would be to make ourselves as small of a target as possible."

Scottie scoffed. "Of course, *you'd* say that. We need to protect our home, damn it!" He stomped his foot and renewed his glare. "Not be a coward."

"Scottie, enough. It's not cowardly to avoid a conflict. I think you've been playing too many video games again."

"I haven't been playing *any* video games."

"Well then, maybe you're going through withdrawal, but my point still stands. This isn't a game. We don't have to act like murder hobos here. Though I do think we should know what we're dealing with. Otherwise, we're just going to be on edge indefinitely. We need to know if it's a threat, and we need to know when they leave. I suggest we find an inconspicuous window and watch."

Scottie huffed, but then nodded.

"Excellent strategy," Thom said as he dropped his arms to his sides. "We might get a better view and be less visible on the second floor."

Jess sighed. "Fine. We can use my room." She turned on her heel and left. A loud din followed her up the stairs and when she turned around, she found the entire household entering her bedroom. She shook her head, then focused on the window she'd been avoiding only a short while ago.

The blinds were down, and she was careful not to move them as she peeked out. It was hard to see through the slats, but she could see the fence, the base of a tree, and lots of grass. No alien, though. She turned, facing the crowd. Melissa, Inez, and Amanda were near the doorway, with Melissa wrapping an arm around the other two women supportively. She could see that Melissa wanted nothing to do with comforting the two, but felt like she had to. Yearning filled her eyes as she watched Jess, Thom, and Scottie crowd around the window.

"By the tree," Inez whispered, barely audible.

Jess nodded, then turned back around, focusing in on the tree. At first, she saw nothing. No movement, just a quiet side yard in the quiet morning hours. There was no one visible at all.

But then she started noticing the shadows and spotted one that didn't fit. It was long and skinny. At first, she thought it was a branch, but the movement wasn't right. Too sinuous. Too curvy.

"Motherfucker," she said as she pushed back from the window.

"Jess?" someone asked, but she wasn't paying attention anymore.

"I'm gonna kill him."

She stormed out of the room, ran down the stairs, and threw open the front door, half expecting the doorknob to embed itself in the wall as she ran across the grass, then turned as she hit the corner.

She spotted him immediately. He was behind the tree, unmistakable, his long tail waving back and forth and giving him away. "You motherfucker! You lied!"

She was on him in a blink. She didn't even remember the intervening distance. One moment, she spotted him and the next, she was swinging.

EPISODE SIXTEEN

The Light of Day

*D*avin was immediately happy as Jess approached, the urge to go to her overwhelming.

A moment later, pain flared through his head, giving him a brief moment of clarity. He looked down, confused at the pure rage staring up at him.

But like a cloud that had only briefly been dispelled by a gust, his instincts slowly took control again. Only this time, he was more aware of it. He struggled to focus, to take in enough information to know *why* Jess was mad at him, but it was hard. His senses were being assaulted from every direction, each new bit of information vying for attention, but none of them were what he *needed* to focus on. He *needed* to focus on Jess, on why she was angry, but some things he simply couldn't ignore, like the scent of several people looming nearby.

Threats.

He shook his head to drive the intrusive thought out, belatedly realizing that Jess was yelling at him. He tried to ignore his nose by only breathing through his mouth, then zeroed in on her again.

"Have you been ignoring me this entire time?" she shrieked, hurting his ears.

"No," he said, but even the brief inhale through his mouth afterward had his attention waning. He jerked his head up and spotted several individuals standing near the corner of the house, spying on him and Jess eagerly.

He growled at them. Some of the tension went out of Jess for a brief moment before it came back full force, and she hit him again.

Davin jerked back, surprised. "What was that for?"

"Don't growl at my friends!"

He looked up over her head at the group of people. There were five of them, and it didn't take long for the little bit of logic oozing into his brain to recognize that none of them was likely a threat. He could easily take each of them out, probably even all at once. He tried to dismiss them from his mind, but it was hard. *Logically*, he knew they weren't a threat, but his mind and body weren't exactly listening to logic at the moment.

He shifted his attention to Jess instead, but that wasn't much better. He could get lost in her, and while a part of him *wanted* to do that, another part *knew* he couldn't. Focusing on her was all he wanted to do. All it would take was a brief whiff, and he would be lost. But he knew he couldn't do that. He didn't *want* to do that. He couldn't *afford* to.

Suddenly, his attention was jarred from his internal struggles when Jess grabbed the front of his shirt, dragging him down to her level. "Hey! I was talking to you!"

"I'm sorry. What did you say?"

She frowned, let go, then took a step back, her eyes looking tired. "I said, 'What are you doing here?'"

His mind scrambled for the right thing to say, but impulses rather than words came to mind. It took him precious moments to translate those impulses into words. "I needed to know you were okay," he said finally.

She scoffed, relaxing her grip slightly. "Bullshit! You said you were going to focus on your mission. You lied!"

He looked away. "I couldn't help myself."

"That's not good enough. You have a mission to complete. You have people counting on you. Does anyone even know you're here?"

He shook his head and cringed, the mention of his team finally making him realize the day had dawned. He didn't know when it had happened, but the sky was now a light blue, most of the flamboyant colors of sunrise long gone. Though the sun was not yet visible over the trees, there was no kidding himself. The gloom of night was no more.

They're probably awake now.

Heat burned under his scales. He'd told himself he would be back before they woke. He couldn't even get *that* right. What the hell was happening to him?

Davin looked around himself, trying to recall why he hadn't turned back. He'd told himself he would just check to make sure she was okay, then go back to the shuttle. He remembered reaching her home, confirming to himself that Jess had arrived safely, but most of the rest of the night was a bit of a blur. Why had he stayed around? Why hadn't he gone back to the shuttle? He had this vague sense of a tug of war inside himself, but couldn't quite fathom why he hadn't done what he was supposed to do in the first place.

Van is probably furious with me.

Embarrassed, he looked back down at Jess. She was furious with him as well.

"I'm sorry."

He wondered what he could do to fix this, to make it up to her, and now, for the first time, he truly understood the full breadth of why people took the anti-mating medications. There was *nothing* worse than disappointing his mate, and he couldn't seem to *stop* doing it. He couldn't control himself, and that was all a normal part of biological mating, wasn't it? Because of the mating, his mind and body were on entirely different trajectories. His mind, when it was clear enough, was often in utter chaos, knowing full well that he needed to get a hold of himself while also feeling the pull of the mating screaming at him. Meanwhile, his body just calmly ignored those muted pleas for logic to reign, instead barreling forward wherever his instincts drew him, like his brain wasn't even involved in the process. He didn't know what to do. He didn't know how to fix this. But he *had* to fix this. He couldn't keep going on like this.

He sighed. "I am *so* sorry," he said again, this time reaching out and holding her hands in his own, hoping his sincerity would get through. "I *never* want to let you down. Ever."

***

Jess frowned up at Davin, realizing for the first time just how much taller than her he was. It was honestly the first annoying part about him she'd discovered, and damn it, she found it endearing for some stupid reason.

Not helpful.

She turned around, taking in the way her friends were watching like it was a soap opera, and shook her head, then tried to shoo them away. She could see the curiosity in each of their expressions, some more eager than others. Scottie, for example, looked like he was about to blow a gasket. In fact, he was chewing his nails like he was craving popcorn and needed *something* to curb the oral fixation.

Jess glared at them, and one by one they turned the corner and disappeared. When the yard finally lapsed into silence, she turned back to Davin. The tension and anger were gone, leaving only resignation and an overpowering inclination to forgive. She was afraid to speak for fear that those words, "I forgive you," would slip from her mouth unbidden.

Weirdly, she *had* forgiven him, even though she knew she couldn't tell him that. *He* needed to learn, to correct his behavior. No matter how much their mating left her willing to pretty much let him walk all over her, she needed to set boundaries and set this relationship on the right path. With the weird mating business between them, it would be so easy for their relationship to become a toxic mess that was healthy for neither of them. She was determined to keep that from happening, no matter how hard it might be to pull off when every atom of her being was telling her to cuddle him like a great, big teddy bear.

Jess sucked in a fortifying breath, determined to make this right. She *wanted* their relationship to be healthy. Davin seemed like a good person, and while she had no idea where this was going, she didn't want this to end up as the plot for a B rate horror movie. She *needed* to do something to set them on a good path, and every good relationship started with good communication, right?

Okay, here goes.

"You realize what you did was wrong, right?"

"Yes, I'm sorry."

"Sorry isn't good enough. You sent me away for a reason. Would you like to tell me what it was?"

Davin paused, then looked away like a child being scolded. "To protect you," he said, his voice almost inaudible.

Jess frowned. "To protect me. Then why did you show up? If keeping me away was to protect me, then why did you come back?"

"I needed to know you were okay."

"Not good enough," she said, poking him in the chest with her index finger. "Nor does it sound like you're truly sorry. What are you sorry about? What are you going to do to improve?"

"I…"

"Do you even understand why what you did was so wrong?"

"I…"

"Things aren't the way they used to be, where a person could just show up at your house, ring the doorbell, and visit. We're in the middle of a global crisis. Anyone who visits could potentially be a looter, a killer, an enemy combatant. We have no way of knowing. And lurking outside in the yard? That is terrifying and creepy as hell! You scared the living shit out of Inez and sent the entire household into a panic!"

"I didn't know."

"No. You didn't *think*." She reached up and tapped his temple. "You're a commander. You have to think about these things, Davin. And where's you team? Where's Van? Are *they* safe?"

"They're at the shuttle."

She nodded. "Okay, so the question remains, how are you going to do better?"

He looked down at her. She could see every emotion in his eyes, and there were a lot. Remorse. Confusion. Fear. Yearning. "I'm afraid I won't be able to control myself. I tried. I really did. I sent you away for your own good, but then I couldn't sleep. So, instead, I stayed up, trying to get some work done, but I couldn't focus. The longer I was awake, the more my thoughts revolved around you, until the thought that you might not have gotten home safe entered my mind and wouldn't leave. I couldn't let it go.

"So, I told myself I would just come by and check. I told myself I would be back before dawn, before anyone woke up."

"Which you clearly didn't."

He shook his head. "No, I didn't. I couldn't get myself to walk away. It's all a bit fuzzy, but I remember the struggle. I don't think I could walk away no matter how much I wanted to."

She sighed, the last of her ire completely gone, replaced by empathy. "What are we gonna do?"

"I don't know. I want to tell you I won't do it again, but I'm afraid that would be a lie. I honestly thought I could before. It was a little easier when you were farther away. My mind was clearer. I thought if my mind was clearer, then I could control myself better, but I was wrong. I had no idea how hard this would be."

"But isn't it part of your culture?"

"I guess I'd never taken it that seriously. I'd hardly ever even thought about it. For me, getting away from my busy family and advancing my career were my main focuses." He looked away, frowning in thought. "If I'm being honest with myself, I always just thought that the people who seemed to lose all control had let themselves get that way. I'd told myself that they'd thrown themselves into the feeling of being mated, and *that* was why they had no control. After all, plenty of people reject matings when they happen, even without medication."

"Okay, then why didn't you take the medication?"

He glanced off to the side, thinking for several moments. "I guess part of it was that my parents had a biological mating, but also, military personnel rarely take the medication. It's a risk, but there are side effects if you do, so most don't."

Jess frowned. "Wouldn't the general public care about the side effects, too?"

He shrugged. "Some do, but most don't. It's the type of thing that matters more in situations where survival is all that matters, not in modern society. Fight or flight responses, stamina, muscle development. It doesn't really affect the average citizen, but those things can be actively harmful to people in the military."

That's odd.

She nodded slowly, wondering why an anti-mating drug would have those types of side effects. They seemed very specific, and like nothing she would have anticipated. She could have imagined fertility issues, maybe. Though she supposed testosterone *was* associated with muscle development and stamina in humans, so it *could* make some sense.

"Okay. So, where do we go from here?"

"I don't know. I thought staying away would help, and I was wrong. What do you think I should do?"

Jess sighed. She wanted to help, to have all the answers and be able to tell him the best course of action, but she didn't know either.

Then again, maybe she was overcomplicating this. Maybe she should be thinking of it as a normal relationship. So then, what advice would she give in a *normal* relationship? If she took the mating out of it, what would be the right course of action?

"Okay," she said, nodding her head as she started to organize her thoughts. "I'll give it a shot. I guess… you have to do what you say. If you don't, I can't trust you, and I need to trust your word if this is going to work."

"How do I do that when I can't even trust my own body anymore?"

She frowned. She could relate, but there had to be a solution, right? Presumably, plenty of people on his home planet made this work. They could too, even if it *was* in some rather extraordinary circumstances. They just had to not set unreasonable expectations.

"I don't know," she said, shaking her head again. "I guess just don't make promises you're not sure you can keep?"

He nodded. "Anything else?"

"Don't creep outside my house anymore. Just knock on the door, okay?"

He nodded again. "Anything else?"

Jess's mind went blank. She looked around her, as if her surroundings had the answer, but there was nothing, just the empty side yard dappled in morning sunlight.

Then she remembered how this conversation had started, with Davin lurking and scaring the crap out of her roommates.

What if someone else reacts that way?

She jerked her head to the side, noticing the direct line of sight between their location and the street. Currently, it was empty, but that could change at any moment. She started to feel uneasy, and the urge to flee gripped her. What if someone saw Davin and assumed he was an invading alien and not a good one? What if they attacked him? What if they somehow blamed her and her roommates, thinking they were working with the enemy? Anything could happen in times like this.

Her skin grew cold, and she rubbed her arms, swiftly deciding they needed to get out of sight. "Come on," she said, reaching out a hand. "I'll introduce you to my friends."

As he gripped her hand, his big, warm paw swallowing up her own, a new worry started to filter into her brain.

What if they don't like him?

EPISODE SEVENTEEN

Meeting the Friends

The moment Jess took his hand, he was ensnared. He could think of nothing else. Her warmth. The gentle lines of her fingers against his scales. The way her hand felt so petite inside his own.

He was dimly aware of his surroundings. First, the change in footing. Soft and steady to hard and uneven. It tried to draw his attention away to his balance, but he resisted.

Then there was a sound, one he'd heard before, but couldn't remember where. They moved into the shadows, and he finally looked up. They'd stepped inside the back door of her home. It was a room he'd glimpsed before for only a moment in darkness. Now, in the light of day, with morning light streaming through the many windows and glass doors, he could see it clearly. It was a food prep area.

But Jess didn't stop there. Still gripping his hand, she pulled Davin forward, and he followed meekly behind, taking in this little bit of suburbia that reminded him of home. The furnishings and architecture were obviously different, but he could see the echoes of his own world in their common purposes.

They passed through a common eating area, then a foyer for receiving guests, before entering a lounging area where the people he'd seen earlier were eagerly watching the window and muttering amongst themselves.

It was a scene unlike anything he had ever experienced. Everything was a bit smaller in scale than he was used to. Central dining and lounging areas on Koa would have had enough space to fit a few dozen people, generally speaking. Here, they would be lucky to fit even a *single* dozen in the small space. As is, there were a total of seven, and it was already crowded.

"Jess," someone said, "What the hell is going on?"

"What's *he* doing here?"

"Why would you bring him in here?"

Chaotically, several voices chimed in all at once, making it impossible for him to differentiate them. His gaze darted from face to face, before finally shifting to Jess at his side, hoping she would take the lead. She knew these people, after all, and probably knew the best way to handle them.

He didn't.

"Guys, stop! Jeez. I'm only one person."

A man stepped forward, fortunately not the one that had tainted his mate's scent. "What is he doing here, Jess?" He crossed his arms, clearly attempting to look tough, but it fell flat. He was the tallest of the group, other than Davin, but he could tell just by looking at him that he wasn't a fighter. The other man looked more like a fighter, but the way he was biting his nails made that possibility highly unlikely.

"Oh, come on, guys. Use your brains. I couldn't leave him out there where anyone could see him. Not right *now*."

"Why the hell not?" someone said, though because he was paying attention to the tall man, he didn't notice who spoke.

"Are you serious? You guys freaked out when you saw him! How do you think someone else would react? I couldn't leave him out there alone."

"He shouldn't be in here either."

"It's not like he's one of the enemy. He's a Drakoan, an ally."

"Then what was he doing outside?"

Jess squirmed, glancing away, as if she didn't want to answer the question.

Is she not proud to be my mate?

There was a moment of pain at the thought, but then Jess sucked in a breath, squared her shoulders, and spoke. "It's complicated. I don't know how to explain it exactly without getting too personal, but it's a biological thing."

"She's my mate," Davin said, trying to help.

"Your what?!" the offensive-smelling male said, his voice squeaking through several octaves before ending his question.

Jess sighed. "His mate," she said as if she was loath to admit it.

Am I imagining that?

Is that what she really feels?

The pain returned, more intense this time, and he reached up, touching the spot over his heart where it hurt the worst.

One of the women scoffed, her own arms crossing in front of her, her stance far more convincing than the tall man. "What the hell does that mean?"

"And why was he creeping outside my window?" another

woman said almost inaudibly, her form partially hidden by the other woman who'd spoken.

Davin immediately felt guilty. This was what Jess had been talking about. He'd disrupted these people's lives, scared them, maybe even hurt them in some small way. None of them deserved that. "I'm sorry."

The room grew quiet for a moment.

"This weakness is my problem, and I let it affect you all. I would say I didn't realize anyone else would be impacted, but that doesn't change the fact that you were. I need to do better, as Jess would say, but I don't know how I'm going to pull that off. I don't know what it's going to take."

"Why did you do it?" the only woman who hadn't talked yet asked, stepping forward away from the others.

He focused on her. "I don't know what all you know about Drakoans, but a part of our biology is the ability to identify a mate by scent. This is very instinctual and driven heavily by biology. It can make rational decision-making all but impossible."

"What does it make you do?" she said, encouraging him as she took another step forward.

"It compels you to be with your mate. Being distant from them is difficult and can even be painful."

Jess gripped his hand, reminding him that they were still touching.

How did I forget?

"Is it always like that? I mean, wouldn't that be disruptive if you could never be away from her?"

"I've never really thought about it. This is all new to me."

"He's doing the best he can," Jess chimed in, bumping him with her shoulder.

Davin looked down, and she was smiling up at him. He smiled back and felt a weight lift off him, making the situation just a little more bearable. "There's a lot I need to figure out. I'm sorry for dragging you all into my mess, though."

"It's fine. I think we can understand." She looked back at the other two women. One was still hiding and trembling slightly, the other looked a little defensive, probably being protective of her friend, which he respected. "So you didn't have a choice in this? Neither of you did?"

He shook his head.

"That sucks."

Jess scoffed. "And it's really fucking inconvenient timing."

Davin frowned, Jess's statement making him think about his team again. What were they doing right now? Were they worried about him? He assumed Van was pissed, but what about the others?

I'm letting them down.

Van could hold his own, keep the team running, but every time he had to come looking for Davin, their efforts here on Earth were probably ground to a halt. The team couldn't exactly go out to complete their next objective when one of their team members was missing, now could they?

So what do I do?

That was the question, wasn't it? He needed to *do* something, but what could he do? When he was around Jess, he was distracted. When he was without her, he couldn't think straight. It was a "damned if you do, damned if you don't" sort of situation.

Maybe I should stand down.

The thought soured his gut, but it might just be his only choice. Van *could* handle things. He had no doubt of that. It just felt like a failure, and that wasn't something he was used to. He was used to setting his mind on an objective and seeing it through to the end. It felt *wrong* to give up, like he was too stupid to find a solution.

He turned to Jess.

He knew she didn't have the answer. She'd already said she didn't know what they should do, but he couldn't help feeling like any solution would *involve* her. It seemed logical that it would. Maybe they could find that solution together. They could brainstorm, after all. That might help. He was pretty useless right now, but the mating seemed to affect her a bit less than him, which was probably a good thing. *One* of them needed to have their head on straight through this.

Or maybe one of her friends would have an idea. He lifted his head, scanning the small crowd in the even smaller room. There was the man who still had his arms crossed in front of him. He was wearing a shirt Davin had seen often in legal dramas back on Koa. Maybe he could be relied upon to be the voice of logic and reason? The other man was wearing a shirt he recognized as being from the franchise "Star Trek." Wasn't his cup of tea, but he could respect a fellow nerd, which was probably the *only* thing he respected about him so far. Then there was the darker skinned woman currently serving as shield for the skittish one. She would make a good soldier. Maybe she would have some valuable insights into strategy? Lastly, there was the female who stood in the middle of the room. She looked so small and soft, it was hard to believe that *she'd* been the one to serve as peacekeeper. But she'd already proven herself to him, and he could easily see her as the center of any effort that might unfold.

Could this group possibly have the answers he sought?

He cleared his throat. "Maybe we should all sit."

He gestured at the seats. There wasn't enough room for all of them, but Jess didn't seem to mind. She ushered Davin into a chair and sat on his lap. He was momentarily derailed by her curves and warmth assaulting his senses, but then he shook his head.

Focus.

Remember the mission.

He took a deep breath, then watched as the last of her friends sat on the other chair and couch. He found himself starting to idly trace a line on Jess's arm as he waited for the others to settle in. When the last person was seated, now looking expectantly at him, he cleared his throat again and spoke. "My team and I, along with other teams all around the globe, are here to support the efforts of Earth's military forces in the aftermath of the conflict. As I've already told Jess, actions by Earth leadership took out the enemy fleet in space, but there were consequences, including the decimation of the satellite communication network and global blackouts."

A couple people gasped, and he paused while they composed themselves.

"We're here in Washington specifically to reestablish communication with leadership. Then we're to move on to New York. We landed about a day ago and have yet to locate anyone, which is to be expected. We're assuming US leadership went to a secure location at the beginning of the conflict and due to the communications blackout, do not know the conflict is over."

Davin looked down at Jess. "I'll admit, finding my mate has complicated things. I'm not sure what the best course of action would be. I want to keep Jess safe, which would mean leaving her here out of harm's way, but that proved to be unfeasible last night, as you all are aware." He focused on the skittish one. "I am truly sorry for scaring you, by the way. That was not my intention. I believe your room is below Jess's?"

Realization popped on her face, and she groaned. "Oh God, you're right." She laughed. "Well, that puts things in a new perspective." She shook her head, then seemed to relax for the first time since they met. Her hand even dropped from the fragile necklace around her throat.

"Anyway, I am at a loss as to how to proceed. If I invite Jess to come with me, she will be in danger should there be any enemy forces still out there. I am assuming they were all taken out by your leadership's bombs, but I would be foolish to operate under that assumption, especially with something so precious on the line." He leaned down and nuzzled the top of her head, the soft strands of her hair silky against his cheek scales. With a sigh, he straightened and continued. "What's more, even if all the enemy have been defeated, there are still threats out there, threats I might not be able to defend her against in the heat of a battle. I don't know what to do."

"Well, it's not like there's a third option, now is there?" the Trekkie said, rolling his eyes.

Davin really focused in on him for the first time. The Trekkie's scent irritated his nostrils, and the fact that he could smell Jess on the man was an incessant irritant at the back of his mind. But seemingly without any impetus, he imagined him with Van. It was at once the stupidest pairing he'd ever heard of and the perfect one.

Van was a very serious person, but also loyal, kind, and brutally honest. His movements were tense, like he was trying to do an impression of a robot, and he was often pedantic, refusing to go off script no matter *what* happened. This made him stubborn as hell at times.

This Trekkie, on the other hand, was far more relaxed. He wore a t-shirt with a small hole in the front and joggers with a stain in the knee. So far, he'd had a smile on his face most of the time, and he seemed to laugh even when he was upset. His movements were more fluid, having an almost feminine grace to them, though he would never describe the man as feminine in general.

They were such extreme opposites. He couldn't honestly understand why he'd pictured the two together. It was probably just jealousy talking. He probably just didn't like the fact that the man was close with his mate, and he was projecting him onto Van as some sort of coping mechanism.

Then a bell rang. The Trekkie bounced to his feet, saying, "I got it!" then rushed out of the room.

Everything stopped for a moment as everyone focused on the door to the foyer. Many had shifted to the edges of their seats, and Davin had even reached his hand down to his holster, just in case. His mate was here, as were her friends, and he would defend them if he had to.

Should have gone to the door myself.

Except it wasn't his home. He didn't have the right to answer the door for them, and they hadn't exactly asked. He would happily be their shield if need be, but again, they hadn't asked. Jess had quite eloquently explained their situation to him in the yard. He knew the fear they lived with daily. He couldn't imagine that answering the door right now would be a pleasant experience, the anticipation of what threats might loom outside filling the mind.

Davin listened as the door clicked open and closed. No words were exchanged. Then two sets of footsteps walked back toward the lounging area. Davin tensed, ready for whatever came next.

The Trekkie stepped through, an odd expression on his face. Then a moment later, Van followed suit.

Damn.

Time to face the music.

EPISODE EIGHTEEN

The Plan

There was an instantaneous change in the atmosphere of the room the moment Van came into view. Davin was immediately tense. So were her friends. In fact, the only people who *didn't* seem to tense the moment the alien walked through the doorway were Jess and Scottie.

Scottie was looking up at the alien with googly eyes, his tongue practically hanging out of his mouth. She wasn't sure if anyone else was picking up on it, but Jess was. She'd been through this with him more than a few times in the past. Every time she played wingman for him at a bar. Every time they watched Star Trek (he had a thing for Spock). In fact, at this point, she was just waiting for him to start fanning himself.

Van, on the other hand, was completely oblivious, instead crossing his arms and staring at Davin. It was the type of stare that, if they were all kids, would have had someone saying, "Oooh, someone's in *trou-ble.*" Then, after a drawn out moment, he shifted his gaze to the others in the room, and that was all it took. They each scattered like someone was waving a gun in their faces.

He stood there like a statue as they flooded out of the room around him. It was almost eerie, ominous, like a scene from a horror movie.

Why am I being so dramatic?

But when the last person filed out, Van unclenched, focusing again on Davin. "What am I supposed to do here, Davin? We had a plan. What happened to the plan?"

Davin's arm curled around her middle, pulling her back against him. Before, with her friends, she would have been okay with that. She might have even embraced it, but now? She felt the need to be *ready*, to brace herself for whatever came next, and relaxing back against his chest made her feel open and vulnerable in a way she just didn't like.

"I'm sorry," Davin said.

"That's not good enough."

Davin laughed, but there was no humor in it. "That's what Jess said."

Van turned his gaze on her, his eyes narrowed in scrutiny.

Jess just shrugged from her awkward sprawl on Davin's lap.

The scrutiny didn't last long, though. "Where do we go from here, Davin? What do we do?" Van shook his head, looking resigned, like a parent tired of dealing with the antics of a rebellious teen. "What's it going to take to get this under control?"

Davin's hand clenched against her stomach. "I don't know." He sighed. "We were having this same conversation only moments ago, and we couldn't come up with a solution then either."

Van turned to Jess. "What was the consensus?"

"That Davin has no impulse control where I'm concerned."

Van scoffed. "I already knew that. What else?"

She shrugged. "That's about as far as we got. I told him that I needed to be able to trust him if any of this was going to work. That's it."

"Sensible."

"Yeah, but that's just about us, not about you and the rest of your team. Not about the mission. I don't know what to do about that."

"The only thing I can think of is the exact opposite of our original plan. If we can't keep him away from you, then we need to keep the two of you close."

Jess tensed. "But wasn't the entire point that you guys wanted to keep me out of harm's way?"

Van nodded. "It was. I'm not going to lie. There may still be enemy forces out there. It's unlikely, but possible. There's also the possibility of encountering less than savory locals while completing our mission. But if we plan carefully, we should be able to keep you safe. It's not ideal, but I can't think of another solution if Davin is going to refuse to be separated from you."

Jess nodded. "Okay."

"We can use standard protection detail protocols. You'll wear body armor and be in the middle of the formation at all times."

Davin's hand relaxed, and Jess did too.

"Davin, I expect you to keep in constant contact. No more disappearing on me. I need to know what's going on, what your status is. I need to know if you can handle your duties or if I need to step in."

Jess could feel Davin bristling behind her. She ran her hand over his, trying to soothe him. He calmed almost instantly. "He'll do as you say." She turned awkwardly toward Davin. "Won't you?"

"Of course. I know the situation I'm putting everyone in. I know the stakes. Again, I'm sorry, Van."

It was a small movement, but Jess was starting to get better at reading the stoic Van, and she noticed when his shoulders dropped ever so slightly. "It's okay, Davin. It's unfortunate, but I would never wish ill on you. You are my friend. And if she makes you happy, I'm happy for you, even if things are difficult right now."

Davin's arm flexed, curling even tighter against her middle. "I feel… mixed." He leaned forward, burying his face against her hair. "This feels so right, so good, but the loss of control is alarming. I don't like it. I wish it would stop, but I don't wish Jess were gone. I need her."

Van relaxed even further, finally stepping out of the doorway. He crossed the room, then sat on the coffee table across from them. "I've been trying my best to keep this from the others. I didn't want them to experience the uncertainty I've been dealing with. They deserve clear direction and confident, competent leadership."

Jess wasn't surprised when Davin tensed once more. Even without being the target of the statement, she'd felt its impact. It was like a slap in the face, and she wanted to comfort him all over again.

"You're right, of course. What have you been telling them?"

Van shrugged. "Just giving them orders, pretending like your absence was perfectly normal. That's one advantage of military life. You get used to operating on incomplete information. It encourages you to not always question things."

Jess snorted. "Well, that counts me out."

Van turned to her and smiled. "You know, Jess, I think I'm going to like you. I think we could be friends." He looked over at Davin, an unnamed emotion crossing his face. "I *hope* we can be friends."

Jess stared him down. She knew so little about this man. Van was slightly taller than Davin, a little leaner, and his scales a little darker. He seemed straightforward, and she kind of liked that about him, though she wouldn't stretch as far as thinking they could be friends. He was too reserved for her liking. Being friends was about more than just liking a few character traits. It was about connecting with someone on an emotional level, and she just couldn't imagine doing that with someone like Van. If she hadn't seen a couple of his outbursts so far, she would have questioned if he even *had* emotions at all.

She sighed. "What are we going to tell my friends? I can't just disappear on them."

Although, she'd almost done that last night, hadn't she? She'd agreed to go with them without so much as leaving a note.

Damn, I'm a fucking awful friend.

"Indeed." Van nodded, pushing up from his seat.

"So, is it safe to come in yet?" Scottie asked, peeking his head around the corner.

Why am I not surprised?

Van turned and nodded, the signal that started the flood.

Scottie nearly bounced into the room as the rest of her friends trailed behind. "So…" he said as he plopped his butt on the couch, eagerly clasping his hands before him. "You and the big guy, huh?" He had a shit-eating grin on his face that immediately had Jess blushing.

"Yeah…"

Scottie nodded, but the gleam in his eye told her she wasn't about to get off that easily. He wanted details, and he was *going* to get them. He always did. But for now, he turned to Van instead, his gaze dreamy as he took in the alien soldier. "So… what's the plan, Spock?"

Van frowned down at him. "My name is not Spock."

Jess turned, laughing into Davin's shoulder then pulling back to compose herself. Davin looked confused, so she leaned forward, whispering in his ear, "Scottie has always had a crush on the character Spock from Star Trek."

Davin's eyes widened, glancing between the two men with a new awareness.

"It is to me, Boo," Scottie said.

Van frowned down at him, but then shrugged it off. "We are here to reestablish contact with your leaders."

Scottie leaned against his palm. "Well, you're a long way from doing *that*."

Van frowned again, this time crossing his arms defensively. "I'm aware."

Thom, who was standing in the doorway, spoke up. "What have you tried so far?"

Van turned to him. "Yesterday, we tried the White House and Capitol. Last night, I reached out to our counterparts in the human armed forces to provide an update and brainstorm, and they suggested several likely places to go next."

Thom nodded. "In an emergency, the protocol is to separate government leaders to ensure a single attack can't destabilize the government."

"I'm aware."

"They'll likely be underground after all that's happened."

"That was their conclusion as well."

Thom nodded, but didn't continue his line of logic.

"It would be a *whole* lot easier if there was power," Scottie chimed in. "Could contact them directly, regardless of where they are."

Van turned, clearly reluctantly, to Scottie once more. "I'm not so sure about that. The satellite network is unusable at the moment.

Scottie scoffed. "That's not the only communications system on Earth, you know."

Van squared his body to Scottie, his stance growing even more tense. "Explain."

Scottie shrugged. "Internet, duh! Wherever the bozos in government might be, they would have several options for communication, but satellite would only be one of them, and probably not even the one they would have been relying on. Wireless can be temperamental. The best connections are always wired. Stable, hard to hack, and even harder to disrupt."

"You're saying they wouldn't have relied on the satellite network?"

"Oh sure, they would… for communicating with space. And it probably would have come into play when coordinating with other nations. But there's no *way* they would have relied entirely on it."

"So, what do you suggest?"

"If you get the power back up in the region where leadership would be, they can reach out themselves, start organizing and coordinating. Without satellites, they still won't be able to reach out to the ships in space, but it would definitely get the ball rolling."

Van frowned, reaching up to rub his chin.

Jess laughed. "Scottie, you just want to get back to playing your videos games again."

Scottie chuckled. "That too."

EPISODE NINETEEN

Returning to the Team

---

*J*ess felt a little sad as she hugged her friends goodbye. This time was different. This time, she wasn't slinking off into the night. But in a way, that made it worse. Her chest felt tight, and she was afraid she might cry.

I never cry.

I'm not gonna cry.

When she pulled back, she forced a smile on her face, and before she knew it, she was outside, her fingers intertwined with Davin's as Van took the lead in front of them.

"Are you sure about this?" Davin asked as he squeezed her hand gently before relaxing it.

She looked over at him and nodded. "I am. It feels… monumental for some weird reason, like I'm taking a huge step, and there's no turning back, but I'm okay with it."

"Good."

"And you'll keep me safe." It wasn't a question.

"I will. No matter what."

She nodded. "So, what do we do now?"

"Well, I'm not sure. We introduce you to the rest of the team, of course, but after that, I'm not sure. Van has the details on the most recent interactions with Earth forces…"

Jess nodded. "Scottie mentioned trying to get the power back up. Van had seemed intrigued. Do you think that'll become part of the plan?" Jess pressed into his arm as they walked, which was awkward, but she kind of liked it. It brought her back to high school.

"Not at the moment, no. I'm sure it will eventually, but our plan has been and continues to be reestablishing contact. This isn't our planet, our home. We don't have authority here. This is a path forward we agreed on with human military leaders. We are supporting them."

Jess nodded, though she wasn't sure if Davin could see it.

"So Scottie…," Davin said.

"Yes?"

"You two seem close."

Jess smiled. "Yeah. I'm closer to him than anyone else in the house." But then it occurred to her that maybe he thought something else was going on, something… romantic. She jerked away, alarm rushing through her.

They both stopped.

"We're just friends, though. Nothing more. Scottie is a diehard fan of dick."

"A… diehard fan of dick…"

Jess nodded her head vigorously. "Yes. Scottie is one thousand percent gay, Davin." She smirked, leaning in. "In fact, if you'll recall, he seemed more than a little enamored with Van back there."

"Van?" He jerked his head to the side, watching as Van continued forward, not yet realizing they'd stopped. Then he remembered the conversation they'd had earlier, with Scottie calling Van names like Spock and boo. And yes, he'd clearly seen that there'd been *some* sort of spark in Scottie's eye, though he doubted the feeling was mutual.

Jess nodded. "Van. Scottie has always had a thing for serious types. Like I said, he has the biggest crush on Spock, and *that* character is like the epitome of serious."

"I… can't quite picture it." He tried to imagine them together, his mind conjuring Scottie fawning over Van, and Van just standing there looking… bewildered.

Jess pulled back, shrugging. "I'll admit. Scottie does have a tendency to come off as a bit of a goofball at first. He's playful and loves his games and fandoms, but he's no slouch. He works as hard as he plays."

"What's he do?"

"He's an electrical engineer, though I'm not sure exactly what he does. Some sort of design work, I think." Jess frowned, but really, Scottie rarely ever talked about work in any detail. And in the rare instances he brought work home, he was more grumbling about the absurdly heavy laptop he had to lug with him than about the projects themselves.

"Do you think he could be of help with getting the power back up?"

They started moving again.

"I… maybe? Hadn't really thought about it. He doesn't have any connections to the power companies, but he might be more familiar with the technology than most. You'd have to ask him."

He nodded, the motion visible in her periphery.

Jess thought about it, about what it might take to get the power back up. He'd said it wasn't part of the plan right yet, but everything else just seemed so nebulous, giving her nothing to hold on to, to focus on.

To stress over.

"How many people are on your team?" she said, scrambling for a topic that wasn't likely to stress her out.

He looked down at her. "Including me and Van? Six."

Jess frowned. It wasn't a *tiny* team necessarily, but would it be enough? She wouldn't say she necessarily understood electricity and electrical grids that much, but power failures tended to be all-encompassing. And even if they could get the power plants up and running again, would it matter? What if there were parts of the grid that were damaged? Parts that couldn't transmit or store electricity? The enormity of the potential problem suddenly overwhelmed her, and she pushed it out of her mind, instead focusing on their surroundings.

Everything looked a little different in daylight so it took her brain a moment to connect the dots, but she recognized these little cookie cutter houses with too many cars out front.

We're close.

She picked up the pace with a smile, excited to reach their destination.

Slightly behind her, Davin chuckled, but she didn't care. Letting him follow as he may, she jogged to catch up with Van, who she now saw turning toward the little park where they'd landed the shuttle.

Not even a minute later, she had a view of the shuttle itself. She was still halfway across the lawn when four people, all with varying shades of red scales, poured out of the back, greeting Van. They seem like a jovial enough bunch, and she smiled, excited to meet them.

These people are important to him.

Then they all seemed to shift as one and she froze.

A hand touched the small of her back, and Davin's voice whispered in her ear. "Come on. Let me introduce you."

Anxious butterflies dive-bombed in her stomach, but she nodded and let him lead her forward.

What were they thinking?

Were they going to like her?

Would they hate her?

Shit, maybe this was a bad idea.

"Everyone, this is Jess. My mate."

Jess looked up, surprised at the warmth and pride in Davin's voice. Their relationship so far had been build on passion and compulsion more than anything else, so hearing the softness in his voice was a surprise. He was smiling at her, and he leaned down, nuzzling her hair. Jess smiled, shaking her head.

"Mate?" one of them said, sounding incredulous.

"Damn, why not me?" another said, the words coming from the only female in the group.

"Congratulations?"

The last one only laughed.

"Jess, this is Erik, Grace, Lane, and Heath," Davin said, pointing at each in the order they'd spoken.

"Pleasure," she said, nodding in greeting.

"What's going on here, Commander?" Heath said, though there was a slight smile on his face and a twinkle in his eye, like he was looking for a joke to make.

Davin took a deep breath, but didn't immediately speak up.

Instead, Van did the talking. "Jess will be coming with us for the foreseeable future. We'll be switching to protection detail protocols moving forward."

"Why?" Erik crossed his arms in front of him as a snide look crossed his face. Behind him, his tail whipped back and forth agitatedly.

Davin flinched, and Jess reached out, squeezing his hand reassuringly. "Because this is new," she said, "and until we've got a better handle on things, this is the best plan we've got."

Grace smirked, the expression quickly stretching into a massive grin. "Oh, somebody's got it bad."

Davin flinched again, and Jess sighed quietly.

Did they have to give him hell for it?

"That's enough," Van said, drawing everyone's attention. "Be ready to move out in fifteen minutes. Jess, come with me."

She nodded, following all of them up the ramp. They each stopped almost immediately upon entering and started pulling stuff off the walls. Van turned to her with something like a black vest in his hands. "Put this on."

She reached out and grabbed it. "Fuck." It was heavy, dragging her down almost immediately. It reminded her of the leaded aprons they used for x-rays, though maybe not quite *that* heavy. Still, as she slipped her arms through and pulled it over her shoulders, she groaned, not looking forward to wearing it for any length of time.

As soon as it was weighing her down, Davin came before her and started working at the front of it, shutting the opening with a series of deft movements. "There. You're perfect," he said before turning to the wall and donning his own gear.

Jess turned to Van. "Where are we going? Is it a long walk?"

"It will be, but first we have to fly in close."

"It's not close?"

He shook his head. "Don't worry. We'll be at the next landing site fairly shortly."

Jess nodded, then followed them through the shuttle. The first room emptied into a hallway with several doors, all of which were closed. When the hallway opened up into another open area, she froze, immediately seeing a problem. "There's only six seats."

Davin looked down at her and was that a blush?

She wasn't sure. It was really hard to tell with scales, but they did look like they'd gotten darker.

Van turned around. "You'll have to sit with Davin. I'm sorry for the inconvenience. I… hadn't thought of that concern when we'd come up with this plan. I apologize, Jess." He turned to someone, Heath, who had just sat in one of the seats directly next to the front window. "Be sure to be careful as the shuttle is currently over capacity."

"Yes, sir."

It took no time for each of them to take their seats. Davin buckled in, then reached his arms out to her. She sat down, letting his hands curl around her waist. Unfortunately, this wasn't like sitting on his lap in her living room. For one, her options were limited. She had to sit with her back flush to his front, which meant balancing on his thighs instead of across them.

And yet, the longer she sat there, the more his heat permeated her, relaxing her muscles. And the way his fingertips traced little circles on her stomach wasn't bad either.

Then the shuttle rumbled to life, and she slipped, now straddling one of his thighs. It was uncomfortable, her outer thigh now pressing hard into the arm rest, but she almost didn't care because the engine noise was vibrating straight through her, leaving her a bit breathless.

Oh, this is embarrassing.

But at least most of the team had their backs to her. They didn't get to see the way her cheeks flooded with heat.

Then the shuttle took off, and she grunted as the force ground her against his leg.

Damn, should have worn jeans for this.

The stretchy fabric of her yoga pants was just a bit too accommodating. And as she tried to fight against the force of takeoff, tried to get herself properly back on Davin's lap, she just managed to rub herself on him more.

Which was when she realized that she wasn't the only one getting aroused from a stupid shuttle launch. She could feel Davin's erection starting to press against her ass cheek, and now she was doomed. Just the thought of that cock so close and ready had her thinking naughty thoughts that just revved her up even more. She was starting to pant, and now she was actively rubbing against his leg, shifting slightly to get just the right amount of pressure. Davin's hands tensed, but then one arm curled around, holding her steady, while the other slipped inside her waistband. She leaned back, moaning into his throat at the blessed feel of skin on skin.

His hand dived quickly between her legs, finding her clit like his finger was a heat-seeking missile. There was no hesitation, no awkwardness. No, he just went for the gold and had heat blooming for her more and more until she could feel it rushing down her legs and curling her toes. Jess whined, completely unselfconscious as he rubbed her off and she rubbed against him, his hardness somehow thrusting tauntingly along her clothed ass crack. She wanted it closer. She wanted it touching. She wanted her damned pants gone, but then he did something absolutely wicked with his fingers and it set her off, her throat locking up in release.

Gradually, her breathing slowed and awareness trickled in. She opened her eyes as the chill air pressed in on her heated skin. Which was when it finally hit her.

Shit, we're not alone.

Four sets of eyes were staring back at them.

Oh fuck.

I just let Davin get me off in front of his entire team.

EPISODE TWENTY

Signs of Life

By the time the shuttle landed, Davin's team had stopped staring (and commenting), and Jess's cheeks were no longer cranking out enough heat to weather a blizzard.

I can't believe I did that.

But then again, that first time, she'd succumbed in the yard where anyone could have seen as well. Her blush returned. She suppressed a groan as Davin loosened his grip, allowing her to stand as the shuttle's engine quieted and the rest of the team stood up and started heading toward the door.

Jess watched, unsure of herself, as they disappeared into the hallway, Davin's hand on the small of her back the only thing getting her moving. She followed, quickly slipping through the hall, then that back room. The ramp was already down, giving her a view of the environment beyond. They were in a small clearing with mostly pines surrounding them. She stepped onto the ramp, picking up the scent of wildflowers, which were popping up in little patches in the grasses surrounding the shuttle.

No one spoke as they started out, with the one she *thought* was Erik leading the way. He took one glance at his wrist, then sauntered off into the woods like he'd been there a thousand times before. Unease slithered through her as she approached the tree line. She'd never gone into a forest without a clear trail before, and there was no trail in sight.

Maybe he's using GPS.

But then she frowned. They'd said the satellites had been knocked out. She found it hard to believe that the communications satellites would be dead and the GPS satellites wouldn't. So what was guiding him?

Once she broke into the trees, she didn't have the luxury of thinking about it anymore. The ground was too rugged, with too many rocks, roots, and detritus, to focus on anything but where she was placing her foot next. With each step, she half expected to twist an ankle or fall on her face, and she was routinely flinging her arms out to steady herself on a tree.

She had no sense of the passage of time until suddenly someone was grabbing her vest and holding her back. She fell against a warm body and looked up, realizing the rest of them had stopped. Van was conferring with Erik, and she looked back and up at Davin, wondering if he should be joining them.

"Davin?"

"The bunker's well hidden, and it'll be getting dark soon."

She jerked her head up, realizing the faint light that had trickled through the canopy *had* gotten dimmer. And now that she realized *that*, other things filtered into her consciousness as well. Like the soreness that seemed to be everywhere. Shoulders from the vest. Legs from walking. Same with her feet. And her ankles felt like they were one step away from snapping entirely. Her hands felt raw from catching herself on rough bark over and over again, and she couldn't help wondering how long they'd been hiking for.

It had been morning when someone had screamed, alerting the entire house to Davin's presence. Since then, they'd walked to the shuttle, flown an unknown distance, and hiked another unknowable distance. She didn't think it had been any later than noon when they'd started out from the shuttle, but Davin *had* given her a ration at some point, and she'd been forced to eat it while walking.

It had definitely been hours.

Van turned to the rest of the party. "Okay, there's a clearing this way." He pointed off to the side. "We're going to camp for the night, then continue the search in the morning."

Everyone calmly nodded, then at Van's say so followed Erik's direction once more. Minutes passed in silence, then they left the trees for a small, roughly circular clearing. The ground was harder here, without the grasses and wildflowers of the last clearing, and the team quickly set about their work while Jess stood there like an idiot.

Before long, they had a fire, warm food, and bedding laid out. No tents, but honestly, she was surprised they even had sleeping bags. No one looked like they were carrying that much. Then again, when she'd watched them pull them out, they'd looked no larger than a water bottle before they'd fluffed them up and laid them on the ground.

She sat down close to the fire, staring into the flickering flames, as she nibbled at her food. Davin curled his arms around her while everyone else chatted amicably, like they didn't have a care in the world. Grace razzed Davin something fierce about getting a mate before her, but Jess didn't manage to follow any of the other conversations.

Before long, the sun had set, leaving only the fire and a sliver of moon to illuminate the clearing as everyone settled in for the night. Jess lay down as well, but she couldn't sleep. Davin had a hand draped over her side, his breaths even in his slumber, but she just wasn't used to sleeping in the open. The ground was too hard, and she was pretty sure there was a rock under her sleeping bag. It was also loud, and in a way she wasn't used to. She was used to the hum of electricity, the rushing noise of the heat or AC kicking on, the ticking of a clock. She wasn't used to crickets and owls. Or the rustling of leaves in the wind.

And the more she heard those sounds, the more it made her realize that she was *in* nature, with not even the barrier of a tent to protect her. She started imagining ticks and ants and all forms of life crawling all over her skin in the sleeping bag. She shuddered.

It's just your imagination.

But her imagination was now running rampant, and she started imagining *other* things that could slip into a sleeping bag, like snakes and vermin. She clenched her fists in an attempt to keep another round of shivers at bay.

Then her bladder joined the cacophony, painfully full and reminding her that she hadn't used the bathroom in *hours.* Jess stilled, wondering if she should get up and take care of that. She lay there, contemplating Davin's arm over her waist and the potential threats the woods might hold. She wasn't entirely certain where they were, or what type of predators she could expect here. Some places had wolves and bears. Was that an issue here?

But it didn't matter. Her bladder wasn't going to take no for an answer. Feeling ready to burst, she eased Davin's arm off of her and sat up. He didn't move a muscle, and she smiled down at him in his repose. He looked calm, relaxed, like he didn't have a care in the world.

She was tempted to stay and watch him sleep, but that wasn't really an option. She had to *pee*.

Jess got to her feet and glanced around, looking for the best place to pop a squat. She spotted a likely spot not far into the woods where she could hide behind a bush and rushed forward. The moment she stepped into the trees, she was on high alert. It was like a switch had been flipped. Clearing=Safe. Trees=Danger. She listened for signs of movement and life, anything that could mean a predator was creeping up on her.

As she dropped her pants, she was all the more aware of her surroundings, feeling vulnerable. She squatted, leaning against a tree for balance, and sighed at the relief.

She was pulling her pants up when she heard voices.

Huh, I thought everyone was asleep.

She adjusted her clothes for a second, getting everything lined up properly, as the voices continued, indistinct but not coming from camp.

Maybe I wasn't the only one who needed to relieve themself.

She looked to her left, toward the warm, flickering light of the fire, then toward the voices. "Hello?" She took a hesitant step forward, keeping the firelight visible in her periphery. She didn't want to get lost. "Is someone else up?"

It was a stupid question. Of course, someone else was up. She could hear them.

But then maybe it wasn't one of the team. Maybe they were a lot closer to the bunker than they'd realized. "Who's there?" She took a few more steps, but the voices didn't sound any more intelligible as she approached.

I don't think those are from the bunker.

It doesn't sound like English.

They'd be speaking English, wouldn't they?

She turned to look toward the fire once more. Someone *must* have woken up, and in their sleepy haze, they were speaking their native tongue instead of English. She didn't know a word of their language, had only heard it the one time when they were at the Capitol.

She kept walking, approaching the voices, but her steps started slowing. Something felt wrong, though she couldn't immediately put her finger on what. The wrongness made her wish she had a weapon, or at least that protective vest, but she was defenseless.

Then she realized what was wrong.

It doesn't sound the same.

She stopped dead in her tracks, alarm filling her.

It didn't sound the same. She was good at *recognizing* languages and language families. She could often get the feel for their cadences and nuances even when she didn't understand the words. And this sounded nothing like the Drakoans' language. This language was hard, jagged, where the Drakoans' language was more sibilant, soft, flowing.

Those aren't Drakoans.

Those aren't humans.

Her stomach soured, her skin growing cold, and she took a step back unconsciously.

Snap.

She tensed, but suddenly everything was quiet. Too quiet. It was almost as if time had stopped.

Then everything sped up. There was a noise, movement, ahead of her. She got a glimpse of someone, something. She didn't know what it was, but it wasn't an animal, and she was right. It wasn't Drakoan or human either.

Oh shit.

She turned and ran, a scream choking off her throat.

Voices picked up behind her, and the alien staccato bursts of words sent fear rushing through her all over again.

She tried to run toward the light, but as she turned that way, there was a voice in that direction, a bad voice.

Shit, shit, shit.

She turned again, trying to keep ahead of her pursuers. She was confident now that they *were* pursuing her. This wasn't her imagination. She wasn't overreacting. There was no disguising their intent. They were calling back and forth, now on three sides.

Trying to box me in.

She pushed herself harder, but she hadn't even bothered putting on shoes when she'd left the clearing, and she could feel the toll it was taking on her feet. Every step hurt now, and they were gaining on her. She could feel them closing in on all sides, the only open side being ahead of her, but soon, even that wouldn't be true.

They're faster than me.

They're closing in.

They're gonna catch me.

I'm gonna die.

EPISODE TWENTY-ONE

The Chase

----

*J*ess screamed as one of them cut her off. She skidded to a halt, pain flaring up from the soles of her feet as the rough ground dug in. There was a sound. It was coming from them, and it sent chills down her spine and goosebumps up and down her skin. It was all around her, overwhelming her.

She glanced from side to side, desperately looking for an out. She was too panicked to see much, just shapes in the darkness.

There.

An opening.

She dashed to the side, no longer caring what direction she was going. It didn't matter. All that mattered was escape.

As she ran past, she got close enough to see them, close enough that their long, sharp fingers grazed her arm. She sucked in a breath, her mind frozen, expecting pain, but none came.

Her feet were on an entirely different wavelength, carrying her away even as her conscious mind still lingered on that touch.

She wanted to stop, to check if he'd cut her, but she didn't dare.

Stop, and they'd get her.

Stop, and she'd be dead.

As she continued running through the dark, her heart pounded so hard, so loud, it felt like nothing else existed, like that constant, frantic beat was all that was left of her. She was nothing but that heartbeat, and they were going to snuff her out. She just knew it. She couldn't go on like this forever. Eventually, she would falter. Eventually, she would break.

Another blood-curdling cry rent the air, and she flinched. More cries followed in its wake, reminding her of a coyote pack crying out to each other, each new voice just egging the others on until that was all she could hear. It was haunting, chilling, and it made her want to curl up into a ball and cry.

It's them, isn't it?

The aliens who tried to invade.

She didn't know anything about them, but it didn't really matter if it was a human, an alien, or even Bigfoot chasing her. Whoever it was, they were going to catch her. She could feel it in her bones. She was already tired from a long day of hiking, and she could feel her body screaming for a respite.

Everything hurt. Her muscles. Her skin. Her lungs. Her head. Her heart. Everything. She could feel tears leaking down her cheeks. Her breaths sawed in and out over dry, cracked lips. Every step took effort. She cringed every time her foot fell, grinding pain farther and farther into her bones. She groaned every time she had to raise her leg once again, the effort more and more exhausting with each step.

Pretty soon, she wouldn't be able to keep going.

Pretty soon, it wouldn't matter how scared she was.

"Got you," something said as it looped a limb around her torso, yanking her off her feet.

Its voice had a true horror movie quality to it, like it was a monster about to eat her, and she screamed again. She flailed even though she had nothing left. Kicking and screaming, she tried to squirm out of its grip, but talons dug into her, piercing between her ribs. She gasped, freezing, afraid to do more damage. The sharp pain was intense, focusing, and she didn't know what to do.

What *could* she do? Would fighting back make those talons accidentally puncture a lung, nick an artery? She didn't remember much about anatomy, but she didn't need to know much to know all the vital parts were right around where those claws were piercing her skin.

He stopped, and though she didn't see them, she could feel the others approaching, their maniacal, monstrous voices unsettling the night.

She shivered, but couldn't bring herself to move.

They emerged from the darkness, each of them making noises, but they didn't feel like words. It was the same rough, staccato cadence from before, from before the chase, and she realized they were speaking in their own language.

Yet he spoke to me in English.

Blood drained from her face as the significance of that settled in.

He wanted *me to understand.*

He wanted *me to be afraid.*

She shivered at the realization. None of this was making her feel any better. If they wanted her to be afraid, they were going to draw this out. That could be good... if someone was coming to her rescue, but if no one had heard? If everyone was too deep in sleep to hear her screams? It would just mean whatever torture they had planned for her would last longer.

Her body throbbed at the thought, reminding her of the torture she'd already put it through. And the longer she was crushed to this alien's chest, the stiffer she got, and the more sensitive her wounds became.

For a brief moment, she was actually grateful he was holding her up in the air, if for no other reason than that it kept her feet off the ground. The soles throbbed in pain, and she could feel blood trickling across the swollen skin.

But that wasn't the only place with free flowing blood. Her captor had loosened his grip slightly so that he was no longer piercing her. But that just meant the sharp pain had dulled and made it easier to track the stream of blood from the wounds all the way down her torso to her waistband.

How much blood am I losing?

Her skin grew cold at the thought, and she hoped it was from the chill of the open air and not something more sinister and dangerous.

This isn't helping, Jess.

Focus on something else.

Anything else.

She tensed, experimentally moving her limbs, but each was like a lead weight, stiff and awkward. She was going to hurt later.

If there is a later.

She flinched.

Don't think like that.

She forced herself to focus outward, to focus on escape, on the enemies. There wasn't much to see, and their voices had become background noise since she knew nothing about their language or what their tones of voice meant. She tried to pay attention to their body language and facial expressions, though she knew those weren't necessarily universal either.

Unfortunately, the shadows were all-consuming, etching her captors with hard lines that made it impossible to truly see them. She could see neither the color of their skin nor enough detail to erode some of the fear that gripped her. Instead, the unknown caused the fear to clench even tighter around her heart.

Focus, Jess.

Focus on what you can *control.*

Focus on something useful.

But what was useful in a situation like this? What would help her? She thought back to her martial arts training. Martial arts *could* help her overcome a size imbalance in a fight. Size wasn't everything, after all, but she was exhausted and hurting, her limbs awkward and not responding as well as she would like. Even if she tried, would she be able to perform any of the maneuvers? Would it even matter if she did? They weren't designed to defend against aliens. She suspected using her training against aliens was akin to trying to use it against an animal like a wolf or bear. Could it be useful? Maybe if she was desperate enough. Was it *likely* to be useful? No.

Then what the fuck do I do now?

She wasn't the kind to hope for a knight in shining armor to come and save the day. Even though the team was *supposed* to be protecting her, she couldn't rely on them. They weren't *here.*

In the grand scheme of things, the only one she could truly rely on was herself. It didn't matter how much she loved or trusted someone, they weren't always there. They *couldn't* always be there, and sometimes all they could do was pick up the pieces afterwards.

A morbid image popped into her head, one she immediately thrust out of her brain.

No.

That isn't going to happen.

I'll make it through this.

I have to.

But then the alien at her back leaned in, his mouth and a disgustingly slimy tongue tickling her ear. "We've made a decision, little prey. Do you want to hear what it is?"

She tensed and another of those spine-chilling sounds erupted from him, and now she feared she knew what it was... a laugh.

He was laughing.

That can't be good for me...

Jess didn't speak, not sure what to say, not sure what to do, but it seemed he wasn't interested in what she had to say.

"We're going to eat you, little prey, piece by piece." His free hand trailed down, making her skin crawl. "What do you think we should eat first?" His claws dug in, piercing her wrist. She cried out at the sharp pain. "A hand, maybe?" They released, then the sharp claw grazed over her skin lightly, threateningly. "Or maybe just a finger to start? Wouldn't want it to be over too soon." Then he moved his hand. This time his claws ran over her stomach, the sharp points cutting through cloth and causing her to freeze as they touched skin. She couldn't tell if they were cutting her or not. "Or maybe we slice you open and turn you into a buffet. Eat your organs while you're still alive." Another laugh filled the air, and again, the others joined in, the pack thrilling in her terror.

EPISODE TWENTY-TWO

Saving His Mate

A scream rent the air, jarring Davin from a deep sleep. He froze for a moment, eyes open and staring into the dark sky above him. For a brief spell, he heard nothing but the steady breathing of his teammates and the night sounds that filtered in from the wilderness around him.

Maybe it was an animal.

Deciding it was nothing, he pushed the sound from his mind, then turned in his sleeping bag and reached out for Jess. He wanted to pull her into his arms so he could fall back to sleep, but her bag was empty. She wasn't there.

A slice of alarm ran through him, which he tried to quiet with logic.

Maybe she couldn't sleep, and she was sitting by the fire or pacing.

Maybe she had to relieve herself, and she'd gotten up to take care of that.

That was probably it. Davin couldn't remember her slipping off once they'd arrived at camp. He didn't know exactly how often humans had to take care of their biological needs, but it had certainly been hours. He imagined her making her way back to camp even now and relaxed, comforted by the thought.

Just give it a bit.

She'll be back in your arms before you know it.

Then a series of shrill cries echoed through the night, and he stilled.

Instinct started taking over.

In a single move, he was on his feet, crouching in the chaotic mess of fabric he'd been sleeping in only moments before, his mind honing in on certain details he couldn't ignore.

My mate is missing.

Something is out there.

I heard a scream.

He could feel his control slipping moment by moment. He needed to calm down, call out for his team. They would back him up, help retrieve his mate, but he suspected he was too far gone for that. He couldn't even think her *name* anymore.

Time lost some of its meaning as he held on to his sanity by a thread.

Do the right thing, he told himself.

Except, he couldn't remember what the right thing *was*, and his nails were digging into the bedding so much, it was actually tearing beneath his hands.

That's not right.

It shouldn't tear.

He frowned, trying to piece together what was happening, but his mind couldn't quite focus the way it used to.

Instead, it was focused solely on his senses.

The sounds around him: the almost painfully loud breathing from his team, the crackling of a fire, animal noises on constant repeat, scrambling movements of some larger creature or creatures moving through the woods.

The smells around him: the sweat of his teammates, the aromas of their last meal, the woodsmoke, the pines, a vague sense of decay, his mate's scent.

He froze on that last one, his mind zeroing in on it like a lifeline. His hands no longer clenched against the bedding. His lungs failed to take in any breath that didn't include her sweet fragrance. He leaned forward, his head drifting from side to side, searching for a direction.

Before he even realized what he was doing, he was advancing, following her trail. It wasn't a conscious thing on his part, and he couldn't have stopped himself if he'd tried. He didn't want to try. He wanted to follow her, to find her.

Another cry rent the air as he reached the tree line, and he growled, his shoulders tensing with aggression.

Threat.

Mate.

Protect.

He rushed forward, his mind now little more than a series of impulses and single word thoughts. His eyes, already well adapted to the dark, now sucked in even the smallest amounts of light that filtered to the forest floor. As a result, the entire scene before him was bright enough to rival broad daylight, which should have worried him, but it didn't.

Instead, he accepted it as his due diligence and increased his speed.

His mate's scent trail was now so clear, so distinct, that he couldn't have missed it if he tried. There was also something else that had him growling every few breaths, no matter how much he tried to keep quiet.

Fear.

Mate.

Then another scream tore through the air. Instinctually, he knew it was her, his mate. He roared, and for several long moments, he wasn't entirely sure what was happening. He was *flying* through the forest. The distance disappearing under his feet seemed nonsensical, and there was an almost out-of-body experience as he followed the trail of her scent, the direction of her scream.

The screaming continued for several more moments before being cut short. His mind filled with rage, blanking out all other thought.

He roared, and then he had no memory of the intervening distance. Not a sound. Not a smell. Not a sight. Not a thought.

When his awareness returned, he was in a small clearing. There were several bipedal creatures, one of which was holding someone around their middle, their feet off the ground. That was the extent of the analysis he was capable of, even in that brief moment of clarity.

And like the eye of a storm, when that moment ended, all hell broke loose. He roared again and dove into the fray. He could feel no pain. His vision narrowed only to the threat directly in front of him. He swiped out with hands, feet, tail, teeth. Within moments, the sticky, metallic taste of blood filled his mouth, but he didn't care. All he cared about was saving his mate.

He had no clue what kind of damage he was doing. He attacked viciously until the creature stopped moving, then he moved on. Each attack was focused, dedicated, and ruthless, wild yet methodical in its determination to end this current threat and move on to the next target.

When there was only one left, he growled, his brain too hazed with its most animalistic impulses to problem solve. He needed to save his mate, but the creature was hiding behind her, holding her to its chest. It had long claws, and based on the smell of her blood on the wind, some of them had already pierced her flesh. Somehow, her blood smelled different from the rest, and it set his blood boiling.

He roared again and charged. He didn't have a plan in mind, his instincts driving him too hard.

But one moment, she was being held in a threatening grip, and the next, she was underneath him, so it must have worked out.

He sniffed the air, but all he smelled was her pleasing aroma and the equally pleasing tang of her enemies' blood spilled. He leaned down, brushing his face against hers, enjoying the feel of skin against scale and the increasing proximity of her scent.

For several moments, he did nothing more than stay there, reassured by her warmth while his body trembled from the fear of losing her that was only now registering in his brain.

He pulled her into his arms, tugging her closer, more firmly, against his larger frame. She felt different than he remembered, but it didn't faze him as something to worry about.

Smaller.

Softer.

He sighed contentedly. He'd defeated her enemies, destroyed the threat against her, and warmth bloomed in his chest at the thought.

She was safe.

She was in his arms.

Then his impulses starting to slide in another direction. He was tempted to rut her, but he could still smell the stink of fear on her. He wanted nothing more than to rid her of it, so he leaned down and licked her.

His long tongue ran from the bottom of her neck to the top of her forehead before repeating the journey. The gesture was calming, soothing, hopefully for both of them. He purred, his sharply clawed hands running careful, equally soothing circles along her belly and sides, trying to comfort her.

Little by little, his body relaxed, his mind calming down and forming more complex thoughts, pulling in more information from his senses, being able to analyze more and more. It started with simple things like, *Huh, my face feels weird.* Or *why is my tongue so long?* Then it progressed to him finally starting to get concerned about the size disparity between him and his mate.

Jess.

Her name's Jess.

His chest warmed upon remembering it, his hands clasping her to him a little tighter.

Which was when he noticed his hands. Specifically, his nails. They were long, and as he looked around him, he realized they must be very sharp. He flexed his fingers outward, wary of letting those sharp talons anywhere near Jess's fragile skin. They'd clearly sliced through the aliens around them with frightening ease.

But why are they sharp?

And why is Jess so small?

He took stock. Their first time together, he'd dwarfed her, but their torsos had lined up fairly well. Now, her torso seemed to be only a fraction of his length, and her body felt tiny against his chest. He had to contort himself awkwardly just to reach her face. His spine was practically curled into a ball, and he was surprised it didn't hurt.

But why?

"Davin?" she asked, her voice quavering, filled with fear.

That's right.

That's the name I chose.

He smiled, but his lips didn't work the way he expected them to. There was strain, like his lips and cheeks couldn't quite obey his commands, instead feeling awkward, so he let it go, frowning instead.

"Davin?" she cried louder, and he felt her pulling experimentally away from him. He held tight, but a new thought filtered into this brain.

Wait... does she not know it's me?

His heart lurched in his chest, the thought brutally painful.

How could she not know?

How could she not *tell?*

But then all the little realizations he'd been having started coalescing, forming a picture that made no sense. Big body. Sharp nails. Long tongue. Oddly shaped face. Unable to smile.

And then there was how he'd been acting since waking.

His arms curled a little tighter around Jess, needing the comfort of her closeness now more than ever.

What the fuck is happening to me?

EPISODE TWENTY-THREE

He's a dragon?!

*J*ess froze, terrified and uncertain of what to do. She felt like she'd gone from the frying pan to the fire, because while her first attacker had been bad, she wasn't sure this one was any better.

She couldn't see a lot from her position, just lots of scaled flesh and monstrous, blood-soaked claws. Its body pressed against her back, its massive limbs caging her in. Heat radiated from its body, making her sweat and making it hard to breathe. It felt oppressive, the entire situation impossible, and her mind shied away from the truth even though the evidence surrounded her.

But she couldn't forget what had just happened. In fact, it ran on a constant loop in her head. One moment, she'd been convinced she was about to die—to be eaten alive, in fact— and the next, there'd been a massive beast tearing through the clearing. It was dark, and she'd had a hard time seeing it, but she was pretty sure it had eaten a couple of her attackers. Even now, it looked like the forest floor was soaked in their blood. She could feel it squishing between her fingers and soaking into her pants.

Jess bit her lip, trying to hold in a whimper. She wanted to cry, to scream, to wail against anything and everything until the world made sense again. This felt like the realm of horror stories and table top role-playing games, not real life. Monsters weren't supposed to exist, and she wasn't supposed to be here. She should have been at home, with friends. If the world hadn't been falling apart, she would have probably been preparing for her next session DMing, maybe responding to comments on her social media to encourage engagement. The *last* place she should have been was *here*, surrounded by death and a hair's-breadth away from it herself.

But when is it gonna kill me?

That was the question. She was in a clearing, helpless and alone with a creature that had just killed every other living being in sight. And it hadn't just killed for food. Bodies still littered the forest floor, and it didn't seem to be making any moves to save them for later, so what was it doing?

She tried to turn her head, to get a better look, but it was point-less. She could only see ahead of her, which gave her an uninterrupted view of the massacre she'd just survived. Around her, the woods were eerily quiet, with only her pounding heart, his heavy breathing, and an odd repetitive thumping noise coming from behind her. There was nothing else. Even the wind seemed to have died down in deference to this monstrosity.

Time dragged on, and her instincts had her wanting to freeze, to stay perfectly still, maybe even to hold her breath. She had no idea what this thing wanted or why it hadn't killed her yet. The anticipation was fraying her nerves raw. Tears welled in her eyes, and she couldn't hold them back. They built and built, eventually spilling silently down her cheeks, chilling the skin there.

I'm gonna die.

It's gonna remember I'm here and eat me.

I shouldn't have come with them.

I should have stayed home.

Why did I agree to come with them?

She was so wrapped up in her own misery that she didn't even notice anyone approaching until a deep growl rent the air, the monster's chest vibrating against her back and practically shaking her out of her thoughts. She gasped, jerking her head up and around.

Is someone gonna save me?

Again, she was reminded of her limited field of vision when she searched desperately for what had set her monster off, getting eyefuls of leathery skin in almost every direction, but it didn't matter. She spotted several people in front of her on the edge of the clearing and sighed a breath of relief.

She opened her mouth to call to them, but paused as fear made her question that course of action.

What if they're not the good guys?

And maybe the beast forgot I was here?

Maybe calling out will cause it to eat me?

She chewed on her lip, wrestling with her choices, but then a familiar voice broke the silence. "Jess? Are you there?" It was Van.

Thank God.

"Yes," she squeaked meekly.

His gaze immediately narrowed on her under the monster's chest, causing another deep, rumbling growl to fill the clearing. He paused, taking a half step back, then lifted his gaze to her captor. "Davin. Can you understand me?"

Jess froze.

Wait.

Davin's here?

But that didn't make any sense. Surely, if Davin were here, he would have said something by now. He would have been trying to reassure her or stop this beast, right? He wouldn't just be standing there, *right?*

The only answer to Van's question was another growl.

He turned, gesturing for the others to leave.

Wait…

Come back!

Fear curdled her stomach as she watched most of her rescuers recede into the shadows with only Van remaining. Her mind scrambled for something to hold on to, something that would make their abandonment more palatable.

Maybe they're afraid of antagonizing the beast.

Maybe they're just moving out of sight.

Maybe they're hoping to flank the beast.

She took some comfort in that last idea, and the fact that Van was looking at her kindly, a strained smile on his face.

Then he turned his gaze once more to the monster above her, his voice now switching to another language, his native tongue, most likely.

Long tense moments followed, but after a while, she noticed that the growling had stopped and the tension in the beast above her had waned.

"Okay, Jess," Van said, finally turning his attention back to her. "The rest is on you." He took in a deep breath and sighed. "I'm going to have to explain something that might be hard for you to believe, but I want to assure you that none of what I'm about to say is exaggerated."

What the fuck is he talking about?

"How much do you know about Drakoans, mating specifically?"

Why is he asking me this?

Jess didn't have an answer to that thought, and the only way she would know was by asking. But she didn't want to speak more than she had to, not with the monster looming deathly close. She paused, her head tilting up to the chest above her, wondering how much she could say without setting the beast off. She turned back to Van, settling on a whisper. "He told me about biological mating, about the drugs some of you use to suppress it, that it's based on scent, that it can cause you to lose control."

He nodded and sighed. "That is all true, but it is not everything. It is true that we can lose control, fall to our baser animal instincts during a mating, especially early in a mating. But it's more than just scenting a mate and losing control. Biological mating is a part of our evolution. It helped us survive as a species. It helped us *perpetuate* the species. Biological mating allows us to tap into a side of ourselves that is not fully within our control, a side not accepted in modern society.

"Historically, it had its advantages. It allowed us to protect our mates and children. It allowed us to provide when resources were scarce. But it is also not within our control and during those times, the mate you knew is buried deep within the surface, almost impossible to reach.

"I need you to know that he would never hurt you, but also that he has only two drives right now: protect and provide.

Nothing else matters to him, and until you can get through to him, he will remain this way."

She shook her head. "What are you talking about?"

He paused, his gaze darting up quickly before returning to her, his expression solemn.

"The dragon hovering over you right now is Davin, your mate."

EPISODE TWENTY-FOUR

The Aftermath

*H*e's a dragon?

He's a fucking dragon?

Jess's eyes bulged as she processed what Van had just told her. How was that even possible? She tried to make sense of it, but it just wouldn't compute. Sure, there were shape-shifters here on Earth, but they had *rules*, rules that this dragon's very existence broke. They couldn't change into things larger than themselves. Conservation of mass and all that. This thing, however, this thing was definitely bigger than her mate. She wasn't sure *how* big exactly, and she certainly didn't think it was the size of the dragons of lore, but it was still massive.

"What do I do?" she almost whispered, still a little afraid of him in spite of Van's reassurances.

"You need to help him calm down. You need to make him realize you're no longer in danger."

She nodded, her brain now working through the possibilities.

How could she calm him down?

How could she reassure him?

Better yet, what was he being triggered by *now*? After all, if he was still in this form, there must be *something* still setting him off. She turned her focus back to Van. "What would he consider a threat? And what can he sense? What cues is he looking for?"

Van frowned, the expression barely visible in the dim light of the clearing. "I'm… not entirely sure. In theory, every Drakoan is different. What any single person deems threatening will vary. What he can sense, on the other hand, *that* should be pretty consistent. Most of his senses will be heightened at this point, and he'll be very focused on *you*."

So he can probably sense how freaked the fuck out I am right now.

Great…

She took a deep breath and let it out slowly, trying to calm herself. She closed her eyes, blocking out the world, blocking out her thoughts. Time drifted by, leaving her behind, and eventually, she even forgot about the body pressing down on her.

When she opened her eyes once again, she was much calmer, and the idea of Davin the Dragon had settled into her brain. It no longer freaked her out the way it had been doing up until that point. It still didn't *feel* like him, and maybe at least part of that was because she couldn't see his face, couldn't see the man behind the beast.

Well, at least she wasn't afraid, on edge, or anxious anymore, which was progress. But he also wasn't miraculously changing back, either. The bellows of his breath still sounded nearby, and his chest still pressed her downward with every inhale.

And he's growling.

Why is he still growling?

And then it hit her. "Van?"

"Yes?"

"I want you and the team to go back to the campsite. Give us maybe fifteen minutes and then check back, okay?"

He paused, the moment dragging on uncomfortably. "You… think he's feeling threatened by *us?*"

She shrugged, though no one could really see it as Davin had dipped his head down low, even more thoroughly blocking her view. "There's nothing else here."

"Okay." She spotted a little movement, then Van spoke again. "Everyone, move out. Back to the campsite."

Jess sighed a breath of relief.

I was right.

They didn't abandon me.

But then they walked away and silence reigned, not even the night sounds settling in to make up the difference. No, all the creatures of the night still recognized the predator in their midst.

They wouldn't be singing anytime soon.

Davin didn't start to calm down until the fear scent and tension left his mate. He was still freaking out and confused, but knowing she was calm was a balm to his psyche.

And yet, no matter how much of a balm she might pose, he couldn't escape his current reality.

What's happening to me?

He wanted to ask, but his mouth and throat felt all wrong. And who would he ask? His mind, though still quite fuzzy, knew intrinsically that his mate wouldn't know.

Jess. Her name's Jess.

How could I forget that?

He dug his claws into the soft earth beneath him.

And why do I have claws?

Again, he wanted to ask, but he couldn't. He roared in frustration, causing his mate to jerk once more.

Shit, don't scare her.

That's a bad mate.

I don't want to be a bad mate.

He took a deep breath and released it.

Just stay calm.

As he started to settle once again, he realized that he couldn't sense any threats anymore. He'd taken out the first wave easily enough, but then a second wave had come shortly after. And they'd been odd. Unlike the first, they'd just lurked on the edges of the clearing, like they were waiting for the opportune moment to strike, but they never did. So he'd chosen to hold still, his body protecting his mate, rather than lash out. If he'd moved, after all, some of them might have attacked her, which was unacceptable.

And his body was big, impossibly big, so curling around her was sufficient to keep her safe. They could attack him all they wished. He didn't care. He would take whatever damage they aimed at her if it kept her safe.

But they weren't there anymore. Nothing was there. In fact, the forest around them was eerily quiet, like a predator was lurking, and it took far too many moments for him to realize that the predator was *him*.

"Davin?" she asked, her voice quavering a bit.

He didn't like the sound of that. It made her sound uncertain or even afraid, though he knew she wasn't afraid. She didn't *smell* afraid.

He curled his head in her direction and nuzzled her, hoping to reassure her. She gasped, then giggled, and he wanted to smile, but yet again, his face wouldn't cooperate. Even so, warmth filled him at the sound of his mate's happiness.

My mate feels safe.

She is *safe.*

I protected her.

An instinctual part of him felt deeply satisfied at that thought. He'd protected her from the creatures trying to kill her. He'd protected her from the intruders.

But… the more he calmed down, the more uneasy he felt about the whole situation. That second wave had felt… familiar. He'd recognized their scents, the cadence of the one speaker's voice. Why did they feel familiar?

And then it hit him.

I know them.

My team.

Shocked, he pulled back, his body awkward, and finally he looked down, his mind clear enough to understand what had happened.

I transformed.

I shifted.

He was in his Drakon form. As a mated Drakoan, it shouldn't have been a surprise. He *knew* this was a possibility. It was an essential element of being mated. It was the main reason his people often shunned biological mating, after all. In modern times, it was terrifying to lose control like this. He remembered almost *none* of what had just happened. He knew Jess had been in danger. And based on the blood on his arms, the metallic taste in his mouth, and the satisfaction in his chest, he'd definitely dispatched those foes, but he had no distinct memories of doing so.

Davin looked up. Jess was now sitting on the wet ground in front of him. She was covered in blood, looking like she belonged in a horror movie. Her eyes were wide as she took in his appearance, but again, she didn't seem afraid to him.

He tried to talk, to reassure her, but this form didn't allow it, and he growled in frustration, causing her to jerk *again*.

I'm scaring her like this.

He reared back, then bowed his head in shame.

I can't be her mate like this.

I need to change back.

His thoughts darted around in his brain, scrambling desperately for information on how to change back, but either his brain was still too fuzzy or he simply didn't know. He held back another frustrated growl, knowing it would only scare her again.

Why can't you just do it?

Why isn't it instinctual?

Change back already, damn it.

But it wasn't as easy as that. He was definitely calmer now, and he could feel the tension that had driven him to this point rapidly slipping away, but his form had not yet changed.

There has to be a way to force the change.

But he couldn't remember *how*. He'd never sought out a mating as Grace had, and he'd never really researched it either. It was something he was aware of but rarely ever thought much about, and now he was paying the price for his ignorance.

"Can you change back?" she said.

She was leaning forward slightly now, and he wanted to change back more than anything in the world, but he couldn't.

He huffed, then a strange lethargy started settling over him. He didn't know what it was, but he blinked, his eyes growing heavy as well. Then it was like something washing over him. His Drakon form just sort of drained out of him, like paint or dye washing down the drain.

He was himself again, but that didn't necessarily reassure him. Things that hadn't bothered him before were now forefront in his mind, overwhelming his senses. He could now clearly feel the sticky wetness coating himself, feel the ground soaked with blood squishing between his fingers and toes. It was uncomfortable, especially knowing the cause.

"Oh thank fuck," Jess said, and she was suddenly in his arms.

He squawked, but couldn't resist putting his arms around her. "Jess, my mate," he said, feeling like he'd come home.

She just held him tighter, not saying anything.

They stayed like that for several minutes, and Davin's mind used the time to torment him with what he'd done. He'd protected her, protected his mate, but he'd also scared her, and now that more details were starting to settle into his brain, he suspected he'd threatened his team.

How could I do that?

How did I not know it was them?

A part of him hoped that he'd imagined it, that he couldn't trust the chaotic snippets assaulting his mind. "Was... my team here?"

"Yes."

"I growled at them, didn't I?"

She nodded. "I think you thought they were a threat."

"Fuck." He looked down, shaking his head in embarrassment.

"Hey, it's okay," she said, reaching out and cradling his cheek with her tiny hand.

He shook his head, dislodging her gentle touch. "It's not okay. I could have hurt them." He looked at the carnage around them. "I could have killed them."

"But you didn't."

He shook his head. She didn't get it. "If you hadn't been so close, I might have."

Her eyes widened briefly before she pulled away slightly. Alarmed, he wanted to reach out and drag her back, but he didn't have the right. This was *his* fault. *He'd* broken her trust, and he would need to earn it back.

Again.

"I'm sorry."

She startled, jerking her head back to face him. "Why are you apologizing?"

"I lost control." He paused, the full gravity of his actions weighing down on him. "How can you ever trust me again?"

She frowned, but then reached out with both hands, cupping each side of his face. "You have nothing to apologize for, Davin. You saved my life. That alien was going to kill me. He's dead now because of *you*, and I'm not. Thank you." Then she leaned forward, kissing him gently on the lips before curling her soft arms around his head and cuddling him close. "You have nothing to apologize for," she said again as she pressed her cheek to the top of his head.

Davin sighed in relief, curling his arms around her waist, reveling in her kindness and warmth.

Thank you.

They stayed like that for an impossible amount of time, and he refused to let thoughts of the future, thoughts of consequences, drift in. They lurked on the edges of his mind, reminding him of what he'd done, but he refused taint this moment. He would cherish it as if it were all he had in the world.

Because for all he knew, it just might be.

EPISODE TWENTY-FIVE

Surrounded

*A*s Davin walked back to camp with Jess at his side, it felt like he was doing a walk of shame. Sure, he knew that that specific human phrase was intrinsically sexual in nature, but the concept had never made sense to him. Why would anyone link sex to shame? Sex wasn't something to be ashamed of.

No, but losing control like that? *That* was something to be ashamed of. And because of the toxic emotions that were currently swirling around inside of him, he couldn't help slowing his steps and dragging out this brief reprieve before the upcoming and inevitable confrontation. Because while he knew he needed to apologize, he didn't want to do it *now*.

Unfortunately, he had no choice. Once he got back to camp, got back to his team, he *had* to do it. He had to apologize. If he didn't, it would be too late. The damage would already be done. And while Jess might have felt he didn't need to apologize to *her*, he knew the same wasn't true for his team.

"Come on," she said, tugging on his hand. "It won't be that bad."

He frowned and looked down, noticing the strain on her face. Then he looked down further and noticed her bare feet. Her skin was far softer than his scales, and he could imagine there being plenty of things that could irritate her skin on the forest floor. "Do you want me to carry you?"

She smiled, but the expression was clearly forced. "I'm fine."

"Are you, though?" He stopped, grateful for the distraction as he studied her features, looking for the truth. Though he didn't have a lot of experience with humans in person, he'd certainly watched enough of their videos for their facial features and expressions to be familiar to him. She was fairly young, he presumed, without the lines around her mouth and eyes that came with age. He knew there were fine lines that could form or deepen there when under stress, but he didn't see any in the dark. He also couldn't tell anything about her coloring in the dim lighting, but her eyes were squinted and her mouth thinned, something he'd seen plenty of times in videos. It always meant something negative, though he generally needed context clues to figure out exactly what. Anger, pain, annoyance. They were all possibilities, but Davin had his suspicions.

Not answering him, Jess just started walking again, dragging him along, but he didn't let her set the topic to rest. Instead, he quietly focused on her body language and facial expressions. It didn't take him long to confirm his suspicions as her body would tense and her face would grow tighter every time she put a foot down.

"Okay, that's enough," he said after only a handful of steps. He reached out, lifting her into his arms.

She protested, her voice probably heard even from the camp, but he didn't care. He wouldn't have his mate in pain if he could help it, so he ignored her objections and continued toward the camp.

"Davin," she said carefully, "put me down."

"No."

"Davin, I mean it. Put me down."

This time, he stopped briefly. "You were in pain."

"I was fine."

"Your feet were hurting."

"I could handle it."

He frowned. "That's not the same as fine. You were hurting, and I could help."

She scoffed. "You're gonna exhaust yourself and there's no point. I can walk."

He shook his head. "Of course, you can walk. But just because you *can* walk, doesn't mean you *should*. We can take a look at your feet when we get back to camp and decide how to proceed. Until then, I will carry you so you don't aggravate whatever injury you've sustained."

She sighed, clearly exasperated with him. "That's not necessary. And what if more of those bad aliens show up? You'll have your hands full and won't be able to defend yourself."

He smirked, leaning in close. "I think I've proven quite effectively that I'm fully capable of defending myself."

Jess shook her head, her eyes rolling visibly even in the dark, but she was smart enough not to comment further.

They continued walking in silence, and a certain peace settled over Davin. His mate was in his arms. She was safe. She likely had some minor wounds, but he was ensuring she didn't exacerbate them, and he was taking her somewhere she could get them tended to. For maybe the first time since he'd scented her, he actually felt like he was doing what he was supposed to be doing. He was protecting her. He was caring for her. He was providing for her. It was a good feeling, and he couldn't resist the little smile that slipped onto his face.

That smile was short-lived, though, as not long after, they stepped out of the woods and into the clearing where his team was waiting.

He froze, staring at them as they stared back. He could see the mixed feelings on their faces. Uneasiness. Concern. Fear. Sometimes all in the same person. He couldn't blame them. There was a great deal of stigma surrounding losing control as he'd just done. He could see how it had warped their perceptions of him. Even Grace, who had always romanticized biological mating, looked uncertain on how to handle him now.

I hope I haven't destroyed her dreams.

He would hate it if he'd done that to her. While everyone liked to joke about her interest in getting a mate, they didn't begrudge her that interest. It was her choice, her dream, and she was allowed to yearn for whatever she wished. Like everyone in their society, she understood the pitfalls of mating. There had been more than a few times over the years where they'd stayed up late into the night, maybe over a few drinks, and that topic would come up. She was always knowledgeable and surprisingly levelheaded about the entire thing. She definitely knew what she would be getting herself into, but maybe *knowing* and *seeing* were two different things.

"I'm sorry," he finally said after a long silence. He didn't know what else to say. Was there anything else he *could* say? He'd lost control. That alone was unacceptable. But as a commander? That was even worse. He'd let them down.

With those thoughts foremost on his mind, Davin looked away. He couldn't bear to meet them eye to eye, to look at the expressions that told him he'd lost something precious that he might never be able to get back… their trust.

How could this keep happening to him? First, with Jess. Now, his team. He seemed to be destroying the trust of every single person he cared about on this mission. And that realization had him clutching Jess tighter to his chest, needing something to hold onto as it felt like his life was falling apart.

"Davin?" Van said quietly.

He jerked his head up, realizing that Van had crossed the intervening distance and was now standing directly in front of him. "Yes?"

Van glanced behind him, at the rest of the team who were looking on nervously, then glanced briefly at Jess before focusing on Davin once more. "You're okay? You're back to yourself? You know who I am?"

I didn't before?

"I…" How was that even possible? He'd known Van for *years*. They'd risen through the ranks together. He was his best friend. How the hell had he not *known* him? "Yes… Van… I know who you are."

Van sighed in relief, then nodded. "Good. Good."

"What happened?"

Van frowned. "I'm not entirely sure. You were certainly not yourself. You didn't seem to know us. I think you even saw us as a threat, but I can't be sure." He shook his head. "It's possible you were just still agitated because your mate had been in danger. That's… my hope."

Davin nodded. "Mine as well. I can't imagine seeing you as a threat."

Van gave him a tight-lipped smile, then patted his shoulder before turning and focusing on Jess. "And how are you feeling, other than probably wanting a bath?"

She laughed, the sound brief. "Would *definitely* love a bath." She was still covered in blood. Some places, like on her face and hands, the blood had streaked and dried. In others, like her clothing, she was still saturated, and he could feel that sticky wetness against his scales. The metallic smell of blood was still ripe in the air, but fortunately, it didn't arouse more than a mild annoyance, as its strong tang obliterating the much finer scent of his mate. But short of going back to the shuttle, there was little they could do about it. She didn't even have a change of clothes.

He turned to Erik. "Are there any bodies of water nearby where we could clean up?"

Erik looked down at his bracer, working with the interface for several minutes, before looking up again. "There's something on the maps here. It's not close enough to safely go tonight, but maybe we can detour that way in the morning."

Davin nodded his head. "Good."

Then Van drew his attention once more. "Is there a reason you're carrying her?"

"Yes, her feet," he said, lifting the arm under her knees so that her feet bounced in the air a couple times.

"Ugh, it's fine," Jess said as she squirmed in his hold.

"Let me see." Van moved, gripping Jess's ankles and angling her legs toward the fire so he could see better. "Yeah, this is not too bad." He turned. "Grace, could you get me the med kit?" Then back to Davin. "Put her down over there and keep her feet elevated."

They all followed Van's commands. Van was the only one of them with more than first aid training. Everyone in the military had specializations, even when they went into command like he and Van had. His had been logistics. Van's had been medic training.

So, following Van's orders as much as he was willing, he sat down with Jess in his lap, propping up her feet for Van to see.

Van frowned. "Are you hurt elsewhere?"

Davin flinched, suddenly worried. "Jess?"

"It's nothing. Just a spot on my stomach. I kind of forgot about it after everything that happened." She touched the place in question questingly with her fingers. "Man, adrenaline is something else. That hurt like a bitch when it happened."

Van nodded. "Let me see."

She leaned back into him, lifting her shirt up to expose her blood-streaked belly, and he sucked in a breath in shock. There were several nasty-looking gouges in her skin, and he couldn't help reaching for them, hovering his fingers there as a vague memory of smelling her blood on the wind hit him.

Davin had to hold in a growl as Van leaned in, inspecting the wounds.

Fortunately, that was when Grace stepped in, creating a distraction when she brought over the med kit Van had asked for, and Davin was able to regain control. It was a fleeting lapse, but still an uncomfortable reminder of how fragile his composure was nowadays.

Van opened the bag, pulling out a cleansing pad and reaching for the nearest wound.

Jess tensed, and Davin leaned in, whispering into her ear, "It's okay," then started running his nails through her hair soothingly.

She relaxed when the pad made contact, then Van proceeded to do his job. By this point in their careers, Davin was fairly familiar with what Van was doing. Cleaning, disinfecting, applying medicine to speed up healing, sealant, then bandages.

Davin watched the entire process, reassuring Jess with mindless words, until Van finally pulled back and started cleaning up his supplies. Jess wiggled her toes, then tentatively touched the bandages on her stomach, and he could feel how much more relaxed she was after Van's care. "That feels much better. Thanks, Van."

Van nodded. "The bandages are waterproof. Just make sure they don't peel back at the edges."

She nodded, then Van stood and walked away, med kit in hand.

In the moments that followed, Davin slowly decompressed. With the events of the evening finally over, he let out a sigh and focused more on his mate's weight in his lap and his arms wrapped around her. It felt like everything was right with the world now. He had his mate. Everyone was safe. He was surrounded by his team. And as he looked around, it seemed like they were even starting to relax around him again, maybe even accept his apology. Maybe that was wishful thinking on his part, but he didn't see any signs to the contrary right now, and that was good enough for tonight.

Around camp, everyone was settling in once more, chatting back and forth, mostly good-natured gripes about being exhausted in the morning or needing lots of caffeine to compensate. He noticed Heath, who had made the comment about caffeine, hadn't looked entirely dismayed at the possibility of needing the extra pick-me-up in the morning. But then, he'd always been a bit of a coffee fiend, though personally, Davin couldn't see the appeal of the foreign beverage.

"Should we settle into our beds too?" Jess turned to him, the maneuver awkward with his arms still caging her in.

"Do you think you'll be able to sleep in your wet clothes?"

She frowned, then looked down and picked at the material, which was suctioned to her flesh. "Uh, no. I feel so disgusting right now. I'm not sure I'll ever sleep again."

He laughed, but then another possible meaning for her words hit him, ruining the brief moment of joy.

Maybe she's not talking about needing a bath.

Maybe she's talking about something that can't ever be washed away with something as mundane as water.

He frowned and pulled her more tightly into his arms, needing her closeness. He pressed his chin to the top of her head, and prayed she wouldn't forever be scarred by what he'd done, by what she'd seen.

They stayed like that for long moments, and Davin lost track of time until Jess snapped him out of it with four simple words.

"Did you hear that?"

He froze, then started focusing on his senses. He couldn't smell much because the scent of blood was still overpowering. Sight was equally hampered as the firelight illuminating the clearing created a stark contrast against the murky darkness beneath the trees.

So instead, he focused on his ears. Jess had heard something, and human senses were universally weaker than Drakonian ones.

He closed his eyes, though he hated the feeling of vulnerability it gave him, and focused on his hearing. It took impossibly long moments as all the sounds around him came to the forefront of his mind. Rustling leaves, heavy breaths from those asleep, crackling logs on the fire, the squishing sound of Jess's wet clothing.

There.

A shuffling noise.

As he continued to focus, he heard other equally faint noises in every direction. They were by far quieter than anything here at the camp, making them hard to pin down.

"Davin?" Jess said, breaking his concentration. She sounded nervous.

She had every reason to be. He had no idea what was going on, but he didn't like it. All his instincts were vying for attention, but he beat them all down ruthlessly, refusing to have another episode, *refusing* to lose control again.

When he spoke, he was proud that his voice was neither shaking, nor did it have a growl to it. It sounded like his normal voice. It sounded like everything was under control.

If only that were true.

Instead, his tone belied his words when he said, "I think we're surrounded."

EPISODE TWENTY-SIX

You Must Maintain Control

This should have been a good thing.

That's what Jess kept telling herself as they were first confronted by a contingent of human soldiers, then brought to the very bunker they'd been looking for. It should have been a good thing, but as they traversed the halls, she couldn't stop glancing over at Davin. And for once, it wasn't because of the magnetism that had brought them together.

She was worried.

It had all started with that thing in the clearing. She knew why he'd done it, why he'd changed, but it was still jarring, alarming. Even his friends had seemed unnerved by the entire situation, and if *they* were unnerved, how was *she* supposed to react?

And it didn't help that she'd already been shaken by the attack. It seemed like everything she'd been through recently was conspiring to send her into a nervous breakdown. She just wanted to go home, to curl up in her bed and forget this entire adventure ever happened, but she couldn't. She was here. And she had to deal with the reality in front of her.

And that reality was that something was off about Davin right now. He'd been off ever since he'd changed back. Tense and overly clingy, he'd just barely started to relax, to return to normal, when the soldiers arrived, fucking it all up.

Davin had then made a brief noise, which jarred the rest of the team from their beds like a blared horn. Not one of them groggy, they'd quickly armed themselves against the (then) unknown threat, and after a brief stalemate and lots of shouting, Van had stepped in as diplomat to diffuse the situation.

She suspected it should have been Davin speaking up instead of Van, but he'd done little more than drag her behind him and growl during the standoff. While he certainly hadn't been as bad as when he'd shifted, he'd also been unable to curb his aggression and deescalate the situation, forcing Van to take charge.

Now, they walked calmly side by side through the bunker, but Davin couldn't seem to stop gripping her hand tightly. It was almost uncomfortable, but it was also the only litmus test she had on how Davin was doing in this situation. She would glance over at him from time to time, but he gave nothing away. Or at least, she couldn't *tell* if he was giving anything away. She wasn't an expert on Drakonian facial expressions, after all. His lips were straight, his eyes slightly narrowed, but that was all she could tell.

Then, one by one, members of the team were ushered into rooms along the hallway. She tried glancing inside, but each time, the windowless metal door closed before she reached it.

Eventually, it was her turn. One of the soldiers gestured her toward an open door. It contained nothing but a table, two chairs, and a mirror.

Interrogation room.

She turned back to Davin, able to see him head-on for the first time since the soldiers arrived. He seemed stressed, and the firm grip he still had on her hand emphasized that point. Their joined arms were stretched between them, but they couldn't stay like this forever. At least for a little while, they needed to go their separate ways. She could see that he knew that, that he was procrastinating that moment as much as possible, but procrastination wouldn't make the separation any less unpleasant.

"You need to let go," she said, her voice a little thick with emotion. She didn't want to let go any more than he did, but she suspected she was thinking a lot more rationally about it than he was. She knew the government wouldn't likely hold them for long. The Drakoans were allies of Earth, and she was a nobody, just along for the ride.

They'd also been doing nothing wrong, so being brought here to interrogation rooms was probably more because of the situation than anything else. The people here were on high alert because of the alien invasion, and they weren't taking any chances, which she could respect.

But as she watched Davin, as she silently *willed* him to follow her command, he frowned and maybe she'd imagined it, but something seemed to almost ripple over his form. It happened so fast, too fast. And it certainly could have been her imagination, but she didn't quite believe that.

She stared, trying to replay the moment in her head, trying to figure out just *what* she'd seen, when Davin finally let go. She paused, her hand still open between them, wondering if she should do more, reassure him more. He looked pained as he stared back at her, and it made her want to rush up and hug him, to squeeze him until all his cares disappeared.

But that wouldn't solve their problems. In fact, she couldn't think of anything that would solve their problems right now. If she touched him, they would be right back where they'd started, and without knowing exactly what he was struggling with, she didn't know how to reassure him. Their relationship was just too new, and they didn't have time to talk, to get to know each other. With the soldiers looming over them, urging her into the room, she couldn't ask him what was wrong. And so she just had to leave it, had to leave him while he was still struggling. It ate at her to do so, but she had no other options.

So, still watching him carefully, she backed into the room, pausing briefly at the door. She tried to read every twitch of his muscles, tried to guess what he was thinking, what he was feeling, desperate to help him, but it was a pointless exercise.

I can't do anything to help.

She sighed, and one of the soldiers reached forward, closing the door and blocking her view of her mate. Then, a moment later, the distinctive sound of a lock being engaged echoed through the room.

Maintain control.

You have to maintain control.

It took all of Davin's willpower to stand still as Jess was ushered into an interrogation room and the door closed behind her. He stared at that closed portal for longer than he cared to admit, even to himself. Eventually, reality oozed in, and feeling somewhat dazed, he shifted his gaze over to the human soldiers. They were gesturing and snapping at him, looking exasperated, though he noticed none of them tried to touch him.

They don't want to risk the treaty.

That thought reassured him, and not because it made him feel more secure. Rather, it reminded him that he was still in control, that he still had access to all his faculties.

But the reassurance was short-lived, as that realization was swiftly followed by a dull pain in his palms. Not wanting to alarm the humans, he nodded to them and started moving again, but the moment they turned their backs on him, he looked down, awkwardly stretching out his stiff fingers. Four small cuts marred each hand, and he knew he *had* lost control. He'd sprouted claws, and somehow he hadn't even felt it when they'd stabbed him.

How was that even possible?

"Sir?"

He jerked his head up. A soldier was impatiently gesturing toward an open door, and he suspected he'd lost a bit of time again.

He glanced over at the room. It looked identical to the one Jess had disappeared into. A part of him refused to enter, wanting to rush back and find her, but he shoved that part down ruthlessly, which was becoming a bit of a habit.

Feeling determined to get a hold of himself, he forced his feet to step forward, feeling strangely hollow as the door closed behind him. He turned around, staring at the windowless surface as that hollow void deep inside seemed to swell and consume him. For a little while, he could do nothing but just stare at it, his mind blank. He felt numb, empty, cold. Vaguely, he thought there was something he should be doing, but it wouldn't quite rise to the surface of his mind. It was too distant, too nebulous.

I'm pushing too much down.

And yet, he couldn't stop. He couldn't even seem to focus on *why* he should be pushing so much down, but he knew it was important. It was *vital.* Maybe their lives depended on it.

And yet, the longer he stood there, the more the hollowness, the emptiness, got to him. He became antsy and started pacing the room. When that didn't work, he started shaking out his arms as well. He flexed and popped his joints. He stretched and ran through maneuvers.

When the feeling only continued to build despite his efforts, he knew he was losing control. And it was different this time. Last time, he'd just sort of blanked out. He had no conscious memory of what had happened.

But this time? Davin could feel it. He wasn't in a rage or desperate with fear. He was anxious, yes, but he was fully aware. It was disturbing, actually. Just snapping and losing control was terrifying after the fact, but this? It felt like he was slowly losing his mind and there was nothing he could do about it but watch it happen in slow motion.

And he knew it wasn't just his mind he was losing control over, either. It was his body as well. He could feel a sort of rippling sensation in some places. In others, it felt like a stretching sensation, like his skin and bones were being pulled beyond their limits. And yet it didn't hurt. It was uncomfortable and strange, but it didn't hurt.

He looked down and was surprised by what he saw. By everything he'd been experiencing, he'd expected drastic changes, but while his claws were bigger and sharper, he couldn't really see any other differences yet.

Maybe it's fine.

Maybe I won't lose control.

Maybe I can still manage this.

The thought made him smile. Maybe he *wouldn't* change. Maybe it *would* be fine. Maybe he would get this under control, and things would just go back to normal.

But then the door opened, letting in a human in a suit, along with the scents and sounds from the hallway.

There were footsteps and doors opening and closing.

There were muddled conversations.

There was the scent of food, probably from the mess hall.

Then there was the scent of blood.

The scent was faint, and deep down he knew it wasn't recent, but it was familiar. It brought to mind that clearing soaked in blood. It brought to mind Jess being injured. It brought to mind the claw marks on her belly. And then his nose zeroed in on the scent of *her* blood, and instinct took over.

He roared.

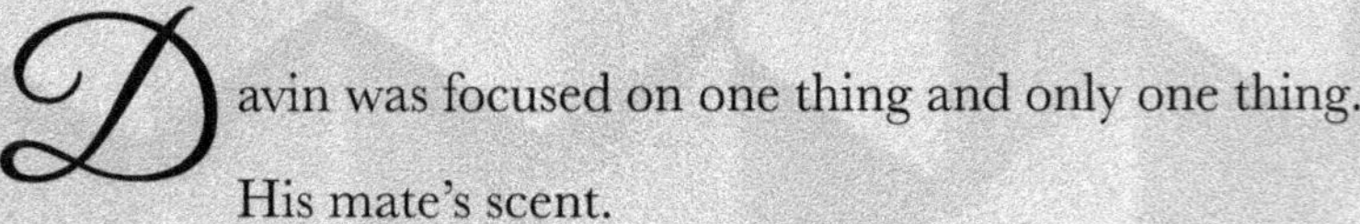

EPISODE TWENTY-SEVEN

On the Rampage

*D*avin was focused on one thing and only one thing.

His mate's scent.

But his environment was chaotic, and only growing more so with time.

Shortly after he'd rushed out, loud noises had started assaulting his ears and flashing red lights had made it hard for his eyes to focus.

What was worse, the faint scent of her blood that had got him moving in the first place was hard to follow. He stood in the hallway, lifting his head into the air to sniff, but then more odors filled the space, obscuring the trail.

Davin roared again and barreled forward, searching aimlessly for his mate. He ripped into anything in his way, anything barring progress in his search. Each dead end frustrated him, making him angrier. Little creatures pointed their little sticks at him, but while he felt things hit him, they didn't hurt or slow him down, so he just kept going.

If they stood in his way, he tore them down.

If they tried to get out of his way, he ignored them, often slamming them into the wall as he passed.

The hallway was really just too small for him. It was hard to maneuver and impossible to avoid anything in his path. He couldn't turn around, and he wanted to scream at the frustration of it all.

Where is she?!

And the obstacles were only growing worse. More tiny beings filled the corridor, blocking his way and making annoying, high-pitched noises that assaulted his eardrums.

Soon, they completely blocked his path. He looked over his shoulder. Even more were pouring in behind him like water filling a vessel.

Why were there so many?

Why wouldn't they leave him alone to find his mate?

Where *was* she?

They continued yelling at him, their tone demanding his compliance, but he'd had enough. He roared at the ones before him, and this time, flames licked out of his mouth. Heat filled the small corridor, and they scurried away like vermin, terrified of being burned. He wanted to laugh, but couldn't remember how.

He continued frantically searching, but he'd long lost her scent. The fire had only made it worse, filling the space with the scent of char and chemicals. His nostrils stung at the feel of it, and he quickly regretted his rash action.

As time dragged on and urgency welled up inside him until it felt like it was nearly choking him, he checked one space after the next, never finding his mate. Some places he searched contained single occupants, the person passive and vaguely familiar, but because they weren't his mate or keeping him from her, he just moved on without a second thought.

They didn't matter.

But with each place he searched, with each moment that ticked by, his hope dwindled until soon, he'd nearly fallen completely into despair. He had been traveling through this strangely smooth cave for so long, and his internal sense of direction was telling him he was moving in a circle. Soon, he would be back where he started. He was sure of it.

But that was when he finally found her.

He plowed through a barrier, shrieking groans filling the air.

And there she was. She was beautiful, standing tall and proud at the back of the room, staring at him with a strength and defiance that made his heart swell with pride.

My mate.

<hr>

The door let out a terrible death cry as it was nearly torn off its hinges. Jess jumped to her feet and tensed, half preparing to flip the table and hide behind it, then a dragon pushed half its body through the small opening that had once been a door. The creature was covered in soot, some of its scales marred by what looked like bullets. There was no real damage, though, the scales looking intact, like the bullets had hit and bounced off. The dragon was red, and because of that, it took her a while to see that he had blood on him.

"Davin?" she asked hesitantly, afraid to even reach out a hand to the feral creature.

He was breathing heavily, but not moving. His nostrils flexed wide with each breath, his sides scraping against the door-frame with each inhale.

"Is that you?"

It had to be him. Sure, there were other Drakoans in the bunker, but who else would turn into a dragon *here?* Davin didn't seem to have a lot of control over it, after all, and she wasn't even sure the others *could* become a dragon. She'd got the impression it was linked to mating.

"It's okay," she said, finally starting to move forward. "Everything's okay." Her mind went back to that moment in the clearing, and she tried to remember what Van had said, what he had asked her to do.

Does he understand language?

Does he know what I'm saying?

She couldn't remember, so she reached out a hand, trying to offer comfort with her actions as well as her words.

As she progressed slowly forward, her breathing was ragged, her hands were shaking, and her heart was pounding away in her chest until that constant beat was all she could hear.

This is all on me.

I *need to fix this.*

Only *I can fix this.*

Even so, she didn't really want to approach. She wanted to run away, but there was nowhere to run. He was blocking the only entrance.

She couldn't escape this.

At least in the clearing, she'd been in shock, so she hadn't been able to really react to what she was seeing. She'd also had the entire team there supporting her. Now? She had no one. She was in a small room with a dragon that she was only *fairly* certain didn't want to kill her. Each step she took was a leap of faith, and she prayed that faith would not be dashed upon the rocks.

"It's okay."

She'd crossed half the distance now. The dragon was watching her intently, but not really moving. He was still in the doorway, still breathing heavily, but he hadn't moved a muscle since plowing into the room.

As she continued to take step after step, slowly but surely, her breathing calmed, her hands stopped shaking, and the pounding in her ears receded. The reality outside the room finally started to filter back into her consciousness.

Alarms.

Shouts.

Screaming.

What the hell did he do?

Then she heard a click, and she remembered.

There's someone else in the room.

Shortly before all this had gone down, a man in a black suit had come in. He'd sat down at the table and encouraged her to do the same. He'd smiled, trying to be reassuring, but she hadn't returned the smile, and their conversation had started in an awkward way, with him asking for little details like her name and profession. She'd known he would eventually get to the point, but then the alarms had gone off, the lights suddenly turning to flashing red. He'd pulled a gun, aiming it at the door, and had encouraged her to duck down. There'd been no time to comply before the dragon burst through the door.

That man was now pointing a gun at the dragon, and he'd just cocked it. From the looks of things, that gun would do nothing more than piss the dragon off, so she stepped into the line of fire, staring the dragon down. The dragon's head followed her movements, reassuring her that she was probably right, that he probably *was* Davin.

But that left one final problem.

How did she stop the man in black from turning this tense situation into an utter bloodbath?

EPISODE TWENTY-EIGHT

Soothing the Beast

*J*ess… was… terrified.

She was facing off against a creature she was only *fairly* certain was her mate, there was a gun pointed at her back, and she felt like this entire situation could explode into violence if someone so much as *breathed* wrong.

"It's okay," she said again.

And in a way, while she might have been facing the dragon in the doorway, she felt like she was speaking to everyone in the room. The dragon, the armed man at her back, and even herself.

"It's okay." She started moving forward, one small step at a time. The beast tracked her movements intently, never taking his eyes off her. Each moment, each step, felt like an eternity in the silence of the room. She could hear each person's breath, could hear the scraping of cloth against cloth, could hear her own heart beating wildly in her chest.

She'd only crossed maybe half the distance when she lifted her arm, reaching out beseechingly toward the beast. "It's okay." She didn't know what else to say, so she just kept reciting that same phrase over and over again like an affirmation or mantra. Maybe if she said it enough times, it *would* be okay, but she doubted it. She didn't know exactly what had happened, but it couldn't have been good.

Then suddenly he stretched out his neck, his muzzle pressing into the palm of her hand. She jumped, but then gulped and let her fingers flex and run across his scales. They felt like leather that had sat out under the sun, and she couldn't help running her hand over them again and again.

"It's okay."

She looked into his eyes, and they seemed both wild and intelligent. Was he more man or beast at that moment? She wasn't sure and couldn't remember if they'd discussed it last time.

But now that she'd reached him, now that she was in contact with his scales, images of him suddenly opening his mouth and snapping her hand off at the wrist sprung into her mind. She shuddered at the thought, but tried to force it from her brain.

That's not gonna happen.

Swallowing heavily, Jess faced the much more likely reality and spoke quietly into the room, never taking her eyes off the dragon before her. "I'm going to draw him into the room. When I do that, get out. Do you understand?"

There was a pause, and she wondered if the suited man was going to answer. "Yes."

"Don't… fire at him. I don't think it'll do any damage."

He cleared his throat, paused, then answered, his voice sounding slightly shaken. "Understood."

She nodded, then, hand still pressed to the beast's nose, started moving to the side and backward. Step by step, he followed her. Time seemed to drag on and on as she continued her constant trek backward. Her every stride felt tiny when using the dragon's own as measurement. Instead of moving his feet, he would stretch his neck to maintain contact. When that didn't work, he would lean forward with his entire body. Only when absolutely forced did he take a step forward, closing all the distance between them in one fluid movement.

Then suddenly, rapid footsteps erupted in the quiet room, disrupting the spell she'd created. The dragon broke contact, whipping his head around.

"No!" she cried out in alarm, reaching out with both hands to stop him from doing anything rash, though the idea that she could have stopped him from doing *anything* was utterly comical. She looped her arms around his neck, holding on for dear life.

Hoping.

Then the dragon huffed, and she realized the room was now empty except for them. The man had escaped. Jess leaned to the side, trying to see around the dragon's body. The door was now sort of closed, and she wondered if they were now trapped inside.

Does it matter?

It really didn't. She'd been locked in here before, so that wouldn't be much different than before. Admittedly, that was without a big ass dragon, but still. She could wait for things to calm down, for everyone to decide what to do.

Though now with the threat of the dragon hurting someone out of the way, new worries started creeping in.

Like what had he done on his way to find her?

Had he hurt anyone?

Killed anyone?

How would the people here, the government, react to whatever he might have done?

The possibilities were endless and had anxiety churning in her gut so badly she feared she might throw up.

But not wanting to face any of that just yet, she buried her face against his neck and just held on tighter.

Maybe it'll be okay.

Reality crept in by small increments. Like last time, he didn't remember much of the intervening time. He remembered struggling for control, he even just barely remembered *losing* that control, but the next he remembered was standing there in a cold room with his mate's arms curled around his neck.

I changed again.

Slowly, he looped his arms around his mate's middle, needing more of her comfort as he came down from the rush of running around in his Drakon form. He shuddered, afraid of what he might have done.

Please tell me they didn't interfere.

Please tell me they had the good sense to get out of my way.

Please tell me no one got hurt.

But he didn't really believe *any* of those things were true. He could smell the blood, smell the scent of cordite and ionic discharge in the air. Hell, he could even smell the scent of fear and piss.

He turned his head, staring at the mangled door. What was behind it? What all had he done? How bad would this be for him? For his people?

"Are you okay?" she finally asked, breaking the eerie silence of the room.

"Yes," he croaked, his throat feeling unused to speaking after even a brief stint in his other form. Then, like a compulsion he couldn't hold back, he said, "I'm sorry," mumbling it into her hair.

She stiffened, then pulled back. He held on reflexively for a moment before letting her pull away.

"Excuse me? You're sorry?"

He took in her expression. She looked flabbergasted, but then it quickly morphed to anger.

"I'm sorry. Why are you upset?"

"I'm upset because you keep saying sorry!" she said, her voice growing increasingly shrill. "I'm upset because you keep *having* to say sorry. It just keeps happening. It happens too much. We barely just met, and how many times have you had to apologize in that time? I've lost count!"

And she was right. He was taken aback by her vehemence, but she was right. He'd lost control, changing into his Drakon form *twice* since meeting her. Hopefully that was something he could get control of in time, but that wasn't the only times he'd needed to apologize since meeting her. He'd made too many mistakes, and he wouldn't blame her if she just wanted to walk away. It was her right. She wouldn't be the first Drakonian mate to do so, and for the first time since meeting her, he *truly* felt the depth of what he was at risk of losing if he didn't shape up.

It felt like his chest was imploding on itself. He gasped and dropped to his knees. He bent over, sucking in great gulps of breath.

I can't let that happen.

If she decided to leave, he couldn't stop her, but he had to do everything in his power to be the mate she wanted, the mate she *needed*. He looked up, but didn't have to look far. Jess was on her knees in front of him, her hands shaking as she reached out to him, worry in her eyes.

"Are you okay?"

He nodded, his throat closing up with emotion. "You're right," he said softly, wishing her hands would touch his face once more. Though even as he had the thought, he realized he couldn't quite remember her doing it the first time. He took in a deep breath, fortifying himself for the conversation ahead. "I keep making mistakes. I'm hoping at least *some* of this is just bad luck. I'm new to this mating, and I need to get used to how it makes me feel so I can finally get some control back." He shook his head. "Our circumstances haven't exactly helped. I don't think I would have lost control like that if we'd met under different circumstances.

"Still, I need to try harder, to do better, even if that means stepping back from a situation that is triggering me. Knowing myself and my limitations is important."

"What are you saying?"

"I might have to draw back from this mission for the time being."

"What?"

"I might have to step down." It felt gut wrenching to admit it, like a failure of epic proportions, but what else could he do? He couldn't keep going on like this. It wasn't working, and they all knew it. But what could he do? What *should* he do?

"Does that mean giving up your role as commander?" she asked quietly.

"I don't know."

"You shouldn't have to do that. You've earned that, right? You worked hard for it, right?"

He nodded, but then he noticed that while the room was quiet, the space beyond it was not. There was a commotion, though he couldn't say what was going on exactly. It was too muffled by the metal walls.

He stood up and walked to the door, Jess trailing behind him.

"Davin?"

"I caused this." He didn't point at the door or clarify what he meant, instead focusing on the increasing sounds of chaos on the other side.

"Caused what?"

He turned to her, a sense of resolve filling him. "I need to fix this."

She frowned, but didn't say anything.

"Will you stay by my side?" He held his breath, afraid she would say no. He was terrified that, without her by his side, he couldn't maintain control, especially in this volatile situation.

She nodded.

"Good. Stay behind me. I'm going to go out there and deescalate the situation."

"You're going to what?!"

But he ignored the exclamation. He could have tried to reassure her, but he wasn't sure if his words would have helped or alarmed her further.

So instead, he turned back to the door, wrenched it open, and stepped out into the madness beyond.

EPISODE TWENTY-NINE

Facing the Music

The hallway beyond was a mess and nothing like he remembered. Dents and scorch marks marred the walls. The chaotic assortment of scents in the air were even stronger here than in the room. The entire mixture burned his nostrils, making him half want to turn back and close the door.

But this was Davin's fault. *He'd* done this, and he needed to fix it. And as he proceeded down the hallways, at first, he saw no one moving, the only evidence of other inhabitants being the sounds of unseen conflicts that echoed off the walls. It was only a matter of time before the stillness around him dissolved into violence.

Still, he had to do it, and he *would* do it… for Jess. The feel of her at his back gave him courage, gave him a sense of peace, like all was right with the universe. Logically, he knew that sense was lying to him, but he latched onto it anyway.

It took some time—maybe because he was dragging his feet a little, telling himself he was just being careful, that he was doing it for Jess—but they eventually turned a corner and the assault on his senses increased. The volume. The smell. There was an open door up ahead, and he could see flashes of movement from within. He approached it carefully, lifting his empty hands into the air before he'd even reached the doorway.

When he stepped through, it was to the madness he'd expected. There was shouting back and forth, each side with guns raised and arms shaking as if they were itching to fire. Van was at the front, his voice lost in the cacophony. He was visibly starting to lose his cool, but trying desperately to be heard, to calm the situation down before it devolved into a shootout.

Davin felt Jess press up behind him, reminding him of what was at stake. He stepped forward, barking, "Attention!" into the room.

His voice rebounded off the walls, the echoes amplifying the sound, and everyone froze. For the humans, he suspected it was an automatic response. One of his brothers was fond of military films and he remembered that word being used liberally in those. For his team, well, they recognized him. They were friends as well as subordinates, and they didn't need a particular word to pay attention to him, even after all that had happened.

He waited for arms to start dropping, for shoulders to relax. People still looked at each other with suspicion, ready and willing to lift their weapons once again, but there were already obvious signs that the conflict was petering out, sanity taking its place.

He took several more steps into the room. "Is this really how allies comport themselves while together? Is this really how we want to represent our respective peoples?" Even saying it made him cringe. After all, he had no idea how *he* had represented his people when he'd changed, when he'd been in his

Drakon form. What right did he have to chastise *these* people? He'd probably done far worse than whatever trouble these souls had managed to conjure up while he was gone.

When they finally grew completely quiet, he took another few steps forward, turning his back to his team and facing the humans in the room. "You may call me Commander Davin of the Drakonian Military. We have come here specifically to provide support in your people's time of need, and I apologize for any misunderstandings that have occurred and any damage that has come as a result of that. Neither of those were my or my team's intentions.

"We were ordered to come to Earth after reports of an amassing alien fleet reached our command. We came here, to this bunker, specifically looking for your leadership so that we could facilitate communications between them and their forces in space."

The humans looked at him, then at each other, never quite fully lowering their weapons. He didn't know how they were taking his words, whether they believed him or not. He suspected the people in this bunker had been in a "shoot first, ask questions later" mentality since long before his team had arrived, and his stupid little speech probably wasn't anywhere *near* enough to calm them down.

Jess stood there with bated breath as Davin tried to talk down the trigger-happy crowd. She didn't think it would work, didn't think it *could* work, but then one of them reached up, leaned his head to the side, and talked into a radio. She didn't catch what he said, but not long after, they were all ushered into a large conference room. Davin and his team were urged into seats at the table, Davin insisting that she sit next to him, while armed and uniformed personnel lined the walls. Their weapons were put away, but she noted that none of them had clipped their weapons into their holsters and most still had their hands around the grips.

They weren't taking any chances.

Time passed slowly. She fidgeted in her seat, checking with Davin then Van, but everyone was stoic and silent. She often frowned, wondering if this was a positive or negative development, but she felt so far outside of her element that she was unwilling to ask, afraid to break the silence that had settled over the room like a weighted blanket.

Then finally, the door opened and a slew of people poured into the room. There was an air of authority to all of them, and she recognized one of them immediately… the President. She flexed her hands against the table, unable to believe that she was *actually* in a room with the President of the United States. How was this her life right now? How was this not a dream?

Then again, it wasn't like she'd ever dreamed of meeting the President. Mostly, she viewed politicians as useless power-hungry fools who would rather bicker amongst themselves than actually do their jobs and solve the country's problems. She went into each election hoping that things would be different and deflating when nothing changed.

Around her, people stiffened, standing at attention as a way of showing respect to the most powerful man in the room. The President ignored this, however, proudly taking his place at the table as Secret Service took their positions around him and various advisors and high ranking politicians settled into the remaining seats.

Then all eyes landed on the Drakoans in the room, making Jess squirm as she was right in the middle of them and felt like the odd man out. She had no business being here, and she felt it now more than ever.

But then Davin reached out and gripped her hand, and she remembered why she'd come.

I'm here for him.

She squeezed his hand back and looked over at him. She could tell he was trying to show a brave face, but that something about this situation was clearly bothering him.

"I'm told you're here to reestablish contact between us and our forces in space," the President said, breaking the silence.

Davin cleared his throat. "Yes."

"What updates do you have on the battle?"

"It's over. There have been no new reports of enemy ships since the bombs detonated."

A collective sigh of relief passed over the room, and the President nodded and smiled. "That's good. That's one less problem on our plates."

"I wouldn't go that far, sir. The bombs presumably wiped out the enemy forces, but they also knocked out quite a bit more. Our ships were incapacitated for a while afterward, and due to sensor issues, we were not able to confirm that all the ships were actually destroyed. What's more, we *have* had contact with hostile aliens since arriving on your planet, so we have reason to believe that not all of them were destroyed in the blast."

The President frowned, but nodded. "Go on."

"I'm sure you're also aware of the power and communications blackouts your planet is facing."

"We're aware. We're in contact with our domestic military bases, so we've been able to get some limited status reports on the situation. Reports abroad are more scattered, but seem to be consistent. I assume you know why?"

Davin nodded. "The running assumption is that the bombs detonated too low, creating an HEMP that caused the power outages. This also affected most of the satellites orbiting your planet. Many were destroyed, some are merely out of service. Your forces in space are currently working on that situation, and unfortunately, I don't have any recent updates on that front."

"But you can contact them?"

"Yes. Our shuttle has a direct line to our ship, which can communicate with your ships in space. It's a slow and arduous relay system, but it works for the time being."

The President nodded. "That's... reassuring."

"Sir, if I may, our directive from command was to provide support, the primary objective being to drive off or defeat the enemy fleet threatening your planet. With that already accomplished, how would you like us to assist you moving forward?"

"I appreciate your offer. And while I have many issues that need addressing, there are three I'm most concerned with."

"I'm assuming two of them are the power and communications outages?"

"That's correct. Those particular concerns have been plaguing us for days now. I don't like the idea of my people being in the dark. In some places, especially in the south, that can be quite dangerous this time of year. People could die without power. I don't want to have that on my conscience if I can help it."

"Of course, sir."

"So first, we need to get power restored, and we need to start providing emergency relief to those areas most affected. I've been working with our military bases to establish shelters and reach out to the surrounding communities. But that takes time, and we are currently out of contact with a great deal of the resources I would normally call on in this type of situation." He paused and frowned. "Second, we need to start hunting down and routing out any remaining enemy forces." He turned his gaze intensely on Davin. "You said you've had contact with hostiles since arriving on Earth. Where was that?"

Davin took in a deep breath and released it. "Within walking distance."

There was a collective gasp in the room, with only Jess, the President, and the Drakoans not looking shocked by his words.

The President frowned yet again, seemingly his favorite expression, and nodded. "That *is* concerning." He turned to one of the men lining the walls. "Take a team and canvas the woods surrounding the bunker. Report back regularly, but I want a thorough investigation. We can't afford to have enemy forces lurking so close by."

The man nodded, said, "Yes, sir," then left the room.

The President turned back to Davin. "You said you have a shuttle?"

"Yes, sir."

He nodded. "I might have a job for you."

Author's Note

Thanks so much for reading Jess and Davin's story. I hope you enjoyed it. Fated Mates of the Drakoan is an ongoing series that I am publishing first as a serial, then as a novel series. Season 2 features Van and Scottie.

If you'd like to keep reading, I've got episode 1 of Season 2 right after this.

Don't be a stranger.

Danielle

SEASON 2: SCOTTIE AND VAN

Episode 1: The Mission Begins

Van sat in the crowded conference room, waiting for just one human to fuck up. They had just been in a standoff together in the other room, and the air was still tense with the emotion of that encounter. Most still had their hands on the grips of their guns, their gazes intent on the aliens in their midst.

He couldn't necessarily blame them. Davin, his CO and best friend, had made an unholy mess of the situation, as he'd been doing since the moment he first scented his mate, Jess. And while Van was tempted to throw the entire situation at Jess's feet so he wouldn't have to look too closely at his friend's behavior of late, he would have had to have been completely delusional to do so. He was just too logical of a person to deny that she'd handled the situation with surprising grace and equanimity.

Which was belied by her behavior now. She was squirming in her seat, her arm occasionally brushing against his own as they waited. Though he, himself, felt no compulsion to move, he couldn't blame her for her inability to sit still. The silence filling the room was enough to make even the most stalwart of fellows uneasy.

And he could admit that he was uneasy himself. Events had gone down that might have long-reaching consequences, and he couldn't help wondering what would happen in the future. Would they be punished? Would the alliance fall apart? The humans were in an untenable situation right now, but that didn't mean they wouldn't eventually hold all Drakoans responsible for what Davin had done today.

He frowned, not liking that thought. He didn't like blaming his friend for everything that had happened, but he honestly couldn't think of anyone else at fault, anyone else to spread the blame to. Davin *had* made mistakes, a lot of them, and he was sure there would be consequences for those mistakes. Consequences they would all have to live with, eventually.

When the door finally opened, he stiffened in his seat, straightening his back and neutralizing his expression. A parade of people in suits poured into the room, a few of them taking seats while the rest took up guard positions around the man at the head of the table.

Around the room, people stiffened or stood at attention, clearly showing respect for the new arrivals.

Then all eyes settled on *them*, the Drakoans, the aliens.

Davin's mate again squirmed, bumping into him. Out of his peripheral vision, he saw his friend reach out and take her hand, clearly trying to comfort her.

"I'm told you're here to reestablish contact between us and our forces in space," the man at the head of the table said, breaking the silence.

Davin cleared his throat. "Yes."

"What updates do you have on the siege?"

"It's over. There have been no new reports of enemy ships since the bombs detonated."

The tension in the room evaporated, and the man in charge nodded and smiled. "That's good. That's one less problem on our plates."

"I wouldn't go that far, sir. The bombs presumably wiped out the enemy forces, but they also knocked out quite a bit more. Our ships were incapacitated for a while afterward, and due to sensor issues, we were not able to confirm that all the ships were actually destroyed. What's more, we *have* had contact with hostile aliens since arriving on your planet, so we have reason to believe that not all of them were destroyed in the blast."

The leader frowned, but nodded. "Go on."

"I'm sure you're also aware of the power and communications blackouts your planet is facing."

"We're aware. We're in contact with our domestic military bases, so we've been able to get some limited status reports on the situation. Reports abroad are more scattered, but seem to be consistent. I assume you know why?"

Davin nodded. "The running assumption is that the bombs detonated too low, creating an HEMP that caused the power outages. This also affected most of the satellites orbiting your planet. Many were destroyed. Some are merely out of service. Your forces in space are currently working on that situation, and unfortunately, I don't have any recent updates on that front."

"But you can contact them?"

"Yes. Our shuttle has a direct line to our ship, which can communicate with your ships in space. It's a slow and arduous relay system, but it works for the time being."

The leader nodded. "That's… reassuring."

"Sir, if I may, our directive from command was to provide support, the primary objective being to drive off or defeat the forces laying siege to your planet. With that already accomplished, how would you like us to assist you moving forward?"

"I appreciate your offer. And while I have many issues that need addressing, there are three I'm most concerned with."

"I'm assuming two of them are the power and communications outages?"

"That's correct. Those particular concerns have been plaguing us for days now. I don't like the idea of my people being in the dark. In some places, especially in the south, that can be quite dangerous this time of year. People could die without power. I don't want to have that on my conscience if I can help it."

"Of course, sir."

"So first, we need to get power restored, and we need to start providing emergency relief to those areas most affected. I've been working with our military bases to establish shelters and reach out to the surrounding communities. But that takes time, and we are currently out of contact with a great deal of the resources I would normally call on in this type of situation. Second, we need to start hunting down and routing out any remaining enemy forces." His gaze became intent on Davin. "You said you've had contact with hostiles since arriving on Earth. Where was that?"

"Within walking distance."

Shock filled the room, people audibly gasping. Van was impressed when the leader didn't immediately react, keeping his composure at the news.

A moment later, he frowned and nodded. "That *is* concerning." He turned, addressing one of the men standing against the wall. "Take a team and canvas the woods surrounding the bunker. Report back regularly, but I want a thorough investigation. We can't afford to have enemy forces lurking so close by."

The man nodded, said, "Yes, sir," then left the room.

The leader turned back to Davin. "You said you have a shuttle?"

"Yes, sir."

He nodded. "I might have a job for you."

Not long after that, the room cleared, with only the leader from before, his guards, and a military officer remaining. Van focused briefly on the dark-skinned officer, reading "Morgan" from the name plate on their chest.

The leader leaned forward, pressing his forearms into the table before him. "I want to first thank you for your service and for coming here in our people's time of need. It is an auspicious milestone in our alliance, and I hope you know that you are appreciated."

"Thank you, sir," Davin said, nodding. "And I apologize for the… commotion I caused earlier."

The leader waved it off. "I'm sure it was just a misunderstanding. I will admit, I am less familiar with the specifics of Drakonian culture than I would like."

"Well then, thank you for your open-mindedness."

He nodded, his gaze scanning over the entire team, then sighed, some of the presence he'd shown earlier falling away as he lifted a hand to rub at his eyes wearily. "I certainly never expected I'd be handling a situation like *this* when I ran for president." He chuckled dryly. "I'm not sure *anyone* could have truly prepared for this." He leaned back. "What a fucking mess."

Heath snorted, and Van turned, glaring him down. The pilot rolled his eyes, clearly unrepentant.

"So, getting to the point of this conversation." The president leaned forward, steepling his hands before him. "Like I said, my two main concerns are power and communication. You have contact with our forces in space."

"We do," Davin said, nodding his head. "As I said, through a relay system."

The president nodded. "Good. Can you patch us into that system?

"Sure," Erik said. "I'll need to take a look at your technology to see how to adapt it, but should be doable. Most wireless transmissions rely on radio waves of some kind, so it's just a matter of looking for the appropriate signals."

"Excellent. Then that leaves power."

At that point, Morgan stepped in. "Our power grid operates by maintaining a constant flow of electricity equivalent to the amount required by the populace at any given time." He frowned. "I propose a multistage approach, first tackling the Eastern Interconnection."

"Interconnection?" Van asked, getting more interested now that they were talking details.

They nodded. "Yes. The grid is broken up into 3 main inter-connections: Eastern, Western, and ERCOT. The Eastern Interconnection supports the bulk of the US population, so that'll be our focus for the time being." He leaned forward, pushing a manila file folder toward them.

Van snatched it up, quickly opening it and poring over the information inside.

"That folder contains all the information you'll need to get started. Contact information, locations, etc. Our power grid is maintained by for-profit companies, so unfortunately, there isn't really a central hub or a phone tree for emergencies. I've provided known contacts for management of the various companies for the Eastern Interconnection as well as what areas they service."

The president chimed in. "I would like you to focus initially on getting power to this area specifically. Having stable power would provide significant benefits in our continued efforts to get the country back to normal."

Van nodded, scanning over the file, trying to piece together from the information which company they should focus on.

"Sure, that makes sense," Davin said. "Once Erik familiarizes himself with your communications systems, my team with get in contact with someone from one of the electric companies and proceed from there. What type of resources are we going to need for that? Is this something our team can do on its own or are we going to need specialists? It sounds like the grid isn't homogenous. Are there any parts of the grid that'll be easier to get up and running than others?"

Morgan frowned. "I'm not sure. I am not an expert in electricity."

"Scottie's an electrical engineer," Davin's mate said, speaking for the first time since they entered the room.

Van frowned, an unconscious reaction to even the *mention* of the other man's name. They'd only had a few encounters so far, but each encounter had been... uncomfortable. The man was his very opposite in every way and seemed to insist on calling him Spock, for some strange reason he couldn't hope to ascertain.

Morgan crossed their arms, leaning back against the wall thoughtfully. "An electrical engineer *might* be useful. A skilled employee of the electrical companies would be more so, though it'll depend on what you're working on." They shook their head. "Again, can't say I'm an expert by any stretch of the imagination."

Van latched onto that idea. "An employee, you say?"

They nodded. "I imagine some plants would need very specialized experience."

Van nodded back. "We can check with this…" He leaned back over the file, reading the name of the person listed next to the company he was pretty sure serviced this area. "…Tessa Dale? Perhaps they'll have advice on how to proceed."

Morgan nodded. "That would be my suggestion. She'll have a better understanding of what next steps you can take and who to reach out to."

He nodded, settling back against his seat as a plan started forming in his head, relieved that he might not have to spend more time with that obnoxiously puerile man. Though with his luck lately, trying to escape the man's questionable attentions might be a lost cause.

After the briefing ended, everyone started to disperse. Van stood, his mind already focused on the tasks ahead of him, but Davin grabbed his arm, pulling him back.

"Give us a moment?" he asked his mate.

She nodded and smiled, following the others out of the room. "I'll keep close to the team, okay?"

Davin nodded, his mouth stretching into an almost goofy grin.

How is this my life now?

When the door finally clicked closed, he turned to his friend. "Is everything all right?"

Davin looked down. He seemed uncomfortable, and silence settled between them for several long moments. Van didn't mind. The military had taught him patience, and he'd learned it better than most. Some saw it as a shortcoming, calling him a robot or statue, but he saw it as a virtue. It could be a godsend on missions, and it could be just as useful in day-to-day life. People tended to react too often with emotions, letting their feelings get the better of them and causing problems that would have been avoided had they simply taken the time to think through what they were feeling first. Far too many fights could be completely avoided that way.

"There's something I need to tell you."

"Yes?"

Davin finally looked up, and while he couldn't quite read the expression on his friend's face, some part of him *knew.* His stomach twisted with anxiety, feeling certain he wasn't going to like what happened next. He took a slow breath in, schooled his face into a neutral expression, and fell into a military ready stance.

"I won't be coming with the team on this mission."

Van stiffened at the announcement, shocked beyond words. He found it harder than usual to keep his cool in that moment, his jaw clenching unconsciously to keep his emotions at bay. He and Davin had known each other for a long time. They'd risen up the ranks together, celebrating each other's wins and drinking away their losses. Even though he didn't show it, he cared a lot for the other man, relied on him. Hearing that Davin wouldn't be continuing with him on this mission felt like the rug had been pulled out from beneath his feet. It felt like the ground was no longer steady. He reached out, pressing his hand to the wall next to him.

Davin looked away again. "Meeting my mate has made things very… difficult for me, which has made things difficult for everyone else."

Van's mind couldn't help conjuring up memories of said "difficulties," like Davin disappearing without warning… twice. Or going on a rampage through an ally's stronghold.

Davin looked up again, his expression beseeching. "That isn't fair to you, or to the team. So, I'll be stepping back. The briefing made me realize that I won't have to completely step down as Commander, though."

"That was a possibility?" Van asked, his facade cracking slightly. Davin had been vying for the position of Commander since the day they met. It was practically the first words he'd said to Van. Almost from the moment they became friends, he'd been thinking of Davin as his Commander and him as Second in Command. And with that thought in mind, they'd supported each other, working together to make those aspirations a reality.

How can he even think *of giving that up?*

Davin nodded. "Yes. I've been useless since meeting Jess. You know that. You've called me out on it more than once. Something needed to change. As long as I'm Commander and suffering from the effects of this mating, I'm failing you all. You need good leadership, and I'm just not it right now." He shook his head. "Jess didn't want me to step down, but I just couldn't think of another way. My head's just not in the right place. It's dangerous for me to be in the field right now."

"You could have returned to the ship." Van would have understood if Davin had done that. It wasn't an ideal solution, but it would certainly have been better than giving up his command, right?

He nodded. "I could have, but I just met Jess. That would be asking too much of her. This is her home. We don't know each other that well yet. How could I possibly ask her to leave her entire planet behind?"

Van frowned, not having an answer to that.

"But when they started talking about communications, it got me thinking."

"About?"

"A communications hub. We're currently working on a relay system, but that system relies on the shuttle and our team. Especially with us now having to relay messages from Earth governments, I don't think we can afford any communications blackouts that might happen because our team is currently unavailable."

"Where are you thinking?"

"Maybe Jess's place? It would be temporary, but it could work for the time being."

Van nodded. "You'll be commanding from there?"

"Yes."

"And I assume I'll be running the team."

"Of course."

Van nodded. "Erik is already talking with Earth personnel about the specs of their communications technology. It wouldn't be that much more difficult to set up a remote station."

Davin smiled, slapping a hand to Van's shoulder. "Thanks, my friend. I knew I could rely on you."

But can I rely on you?

Van frowned, the weight of Davin's hand weighing his heart down as well.

<hr>

Want to keep reading? Find out where you can get Season 2 at https://www.theeternalscribe.com/fated-mates-of-the-drakoan/.

And if you're interested, I also have some free content available through my mailing list. I offer bonus epilogues, free books, and how to get free early access to some of my content.

Sign up at www.theeternalscribe.com.

DID YOU ENJOY THE BOOK?

ACKNOWLEDGMENTS

I want to thank the members of my eBook Lover tier on my subscription, Diana Jacobs and Sherri.

ABOUT THE AUTHOR

I am a scientist, a dog parent, and part-time author of SciFi Romance. I love happy endings and using my biology degree in ways it was absolutely not intended. That means a lot of interesting alien biology as well as thoughtful world building.

But that's not the only reason to enjoy my writing. I also like writing diverse characters (LGBTQIA+, neurodivergent, and more) and (because I'm an author and what more can you expect from me?) throwing them into mortal peril every time it makes sense for the plot (which is sadly nowhere NEAR as often as I would like).

If that sounds like something that's up your alley, check out the links below.

reamstories.com/authordanielleforrest

bsky.app/profile/danielleforrest.bsky.social

amazon.com/author/danielleforrest

bookbub.com/profile/danielle-forrest

youtube.com/@authordanielleforrest

goodreads.com/theeternalscribe

threads.net/@authordanielleforrest

facebook.com/theeternalscribe

instagram.com/authordanielleforrest

ALSO BY DANIELLE FORREST

THE DARKEST DAY SERIES

Mila's Flight

Mila's Shift

Tristan's Choice

Terra's Fate

The Darkest Day Collection

A SHIFT IN SPACE SERIES

Shifting Sides

Shifting Cargo

Shifting Loot

Shifting Paradigms

Shifting Tides

Shifting Shadows

MATCHED TO THE ALIEN SERIES

Matched to the Alien Prince

Matched to the Alien Captain (Coming Soon)

Matched to the Alien Workaholic (Coming Soon)

FATED MATES OF THE DRAKOAN SERIES

Fated Mates of the Drakoan Serial

Season 1: Jess and Davin